Delinquents and Other Escape Attempts

"Nick Rees Gardner's *Delinquents and Other Escape Attempts* immerses us in middle America's opioid crisis with raw and riveting stories. Each narrative pulses with the urgent rhythms of lives on the edge, where hope and despair collide in a bang, presenting us with the possibilities of living that one precious life. The characters in these stories are so alive, so real—their struggles, laid bare with stark honesty, are never exploited to gain emotional connection. This is a testament to Gardner's immense storytelling talent. The stories here are firecrackers: you don't know it going in, but you will once they blow and crackle and jump start your unknowing heart back to feeling alive. Gardner has crafted an enduring and indelible masterpiece, a journey into the soul of our shared community of humanity. Simply put, *Delinquents and Other Escape Attempts* is a triumph of literary brilliance, and it is one I will never forget."

–Morgan Talty, national bestselling author of
Night of the Living Rez and *Fire Exit: A Novel*

"Nick Rees Gardner's *Delinquents* is fierce and funny and beautiful. These stories offer a tonal echo of Sherwood Anderson's Midwest, along with Denis Johnson's recognition that addiction and storytelling provide different but related escape hatches. Gardner's sentences destroyed me, again and again. An excruciating, gorgeous debut."
–Emily Fridlund, author of the Man Booker Prize finalist
History of Wolves and *Catapult: Stories*

"*Delinquents and Other Escape Attempts* is an ecstatic, heartbreaking portrait of the opioid-sick Midwest—*Winesburg, Ohio* by way of Jim Carroll's *The Basketball Diaries*. In fiery prose reminiscent of Denis Johnson, yet fiercely his own, Nick Rees Gardner writes of tragic misfits on the verge of salvation, almost but never quite sober, reaching toward the light."

–Kevin Maloney, author of *The Red-Headed Pilgrim* and *Cult of Loretta*

"Nick Rees Gardner writes of a forgotten America, a place of desperation, sorrow, and indelible beauty. Amid a landscape of pill mills and junkyards, his characters attempt to transcend their pasts, and their struggles illuminate Westinghouse, Ohio like flashes across the night sky. *Delinquents* is an essential collection about the other side of 21st century life."

–Maxim Loskutoff, author of *Old King*, *Ruthie Fear*, and *Come West and See: Stories*

"Nick Rees Gardner writes sly, heartbreaking stories about friendship, drugs, loneliness, and food trucks. *Delinquents* is as self-aware and world-wise (or at least Ohio-wise) as an addict in recovery."

–Rebecca Schiff, author of *The Bed Moved: Stories*

"A dazzling debut. Golden with gorgeous language and grimy with the stench of the real. I shit you not, set this down with *Trainspotting* and *Basketball Diaries* and *Jesus' Son* as among the most beautiful elegies to addiction. It is shatteringly strong. It searches for, and finds, that jolt. Highly, highly recommend."

–Brian Allen Carr, author of *Opioid, Indiana* and *Bad Foundations*

"The stories are suffused with a palpable sense of place.... And the prose is alliterative and earthy, making use of streetwise analogies that ground it in realism."

–Joseph S. Pete, *Foreword Reviews*

Delinquents

and Other Escape Attempts

Delinquents
and Other Escape Attempts

Linked Stories

Nick Rees Gardner

For permissions, contact: editor@madronabooks.com

ISBN: 978-1-960593-03-0
Cataloging-in-Publication Data is available upon request

Stories from this collection were first published, in slightly different forms, in the following outlets:
"Psychedelicious," *Cutleaf*, Fall 2023
"Digging," *Peauxdunque Review*, Winter 2022
"Sever the Head," *Gordon Square Review*, May 2022
"Orange Pill, Yellow Wrangler," *Trampset*, May 2022
"Delinquents" (published as "Towards a History of the Opioid Epidemic and the Midwest to Ohio Pill Mill Carpools"), *Epiphany*, October 2021
"Drug Magic," *Atticus Review*, May 2021

"Beginning" by James Wright used with permission from Wesleyan University Press. Source: *Above the River: The Complete Poems* (1990)

Book design by Kevin Breen
Cover art by John Thrasher
Map of Westinghouse, OH by John Thrasher

Manufactured in the United States of America

Published by
Madrona Books, Olympia, Washington
www.madronabooks.com

Contents

Lake Erie

Legend

1	Rust's Rocks	11	Bathrooms
2	Country Club	12	Town Square
3	Susie's Wine Cellar	13	Church of Future Souls
4	Airport	14	Mag's house
5	Prison	15	Literati house
6	Mara's apartment	16	the Cliffs
7	Tequila Saloon	17	Dad Bod Brewing
8	Phoenix Brewery	18	Hospital
9	G&T Bar	19	Robbie's house
10	Worlinger's	20	Campus

Cleveland

State Forest

Cotter's Run

Westinghouse, Ohio

Delinquents

I asked my characters what they wanted and they answered: Oxycontin, Xanax, blunts, and booze. My goal was to write a book about middle America during the opioid epidemic. I ran cars full of dope boys with fake MRIs from Ohio to Florida, where we picked up prescriptions of painkillers from the Fort Lauderdale pill mills to snort and shoot and sell back in Hillbilly Oz. It was immersive research, the kind people sometimes don't come back from.

∽

Dallas introduced me to Oxycontin sophomore year of undergrad. We were taking a creative writing workshop with Professor Stoneman, an exemplar of the old guard who loved his scotch and simple sentences. Stoneman praised our enthusiasm for the machismo-driven underbelly, turning a blind eye when Dallas and I passed a flask beneath the desk and slipped out of class to get high. Stoneman said that in any good story, your characters have to want something. Once they have it, that story is over.

For Dallas and me the tale began when we had the drugs, when we sniffed them from the backs of toilets in Westwood Hall. We got hooked on the stuff together, though. While I held onto my job at the campus writing center until graduation, Dallas dropped out, slummed from apartment to apartment, scraping by on his girlfriend Judy's Cracker Barrel paycheck.

As we both dipped into addiction, I'd started to fool around with the idea of the book. At Cracker Barrel, Dallas and I ate gratis pecan pie and discussed how we could Scarface our way to the top. He wanted to be the hero of my story, called himself the King of Ohio. He said he was going to get a tattoo of the skyline on his arm and below it, *I run my city*. He said, You'll write it all. Preserve our legacy.

I didn't tell him that Westinghouse wasn't Cleveland or Columbus, that *I run this rinky-dink town* would be truer. A writer doesn't interfere with his subjects. I took notes on Dallas's far-fetched dreams and the junkyard, Rust's Recks.

Rust was rumored to have ridden in a twister all the way from Youngstown till his trailer plopped down there in the middle of Ohio. He christened the two acres Hillbilly Oz, then built a barn. The trailer park grew around him, abandoned vehicles in the field. He parted out Jeeps and Hondas in under-the-counter deals. It was Rust who let us in on the ground floor: he'd cover the expenses of the Florida trip, the medical forms and co-pays, the fuel and petty cash, all in exchange for half of our prescriptions.

And then we were off. Dallas and I broke speed limits through the cornfield-stubbled Midwest. We stopped at a Chick-fil-A in Georgia and let the grease run down our chins before we continued toward the shore. So close, but we never touched the ocean. We waited in line at the strip mall, pain clinic sign gleaming, mouths thirsty for the sustained high, a ceaseless supply, an answer to all our struggles. We alternated pilot and co-pilot, down the peninsula and back to Hillbilly Oz, pockets rattling with pain pill scripts which we'd split with Rust and blast off again.

Those were our glory days. Hope and momentum propelled us through recessions and housing crises, through breakups, deaths, wars, and other losses. I didn't even question our precarity until the day Dallas shoved Judy down the stairs. He'd blown through all his pills and when she got on him, he slapped her. She dialed nine-one-one so Dallas pushed her. The operator questioned the gasps, then the buzz of silence on the line.

When I showed up to the Verdant Valley Villas for another carpool to the Sunshine State, I saw the lot swarmed with cops and I bounced.

∽

The last conversation I ever had with Dallas, after he got out on bail, before he OD'd on fentanyl-laced stamp bags from Pittsburgh, he told me that the day he'd nearly killed Judy was the day he saw his soul. Seated at the folding table in my poor excuse for a dining room, he cried into the pecan pie I'd taken to-go, didn't even use the fork I'd shined with a damp paper towel. The folding chairs we sat on were slanted and we kept having to right ourselves, sliding and straightening again and again. We avoided eye contact as he described his epiphany. He said, Look at this clock, and pointed to the plastic ticking disc on my apartment's wall. He said, It's broken. I told him it was just wrong because I hadn't changed it for daylight savings, but he said, No. Broken. Like time itself is broken. Then he collapsed from his chair, thumped on the floor.

I admit I was a bit confused. I knew that time wasn't real, was all too familiar with the whole *time is an illusion* rhetoric we stoners would wield against The Man. What Dallas meant was literal temporal failure. He said that as Judy began to tumble, his own body froze. Everything paused. He watched his soul emerge in a bloom of jellyfish, a great many-tentacled spirit. Dallas believed it was the pills that made it happen, and this jelly cloud was his true self come unbound where his bumbling body failed. The bloom is what kept Judy from death. When she lost consciousness, when her own bloom emerged, the jellies met in an electrified cloud, hummed bolts into her limp limbs to shock her, sent her gasping back to life. So, really, he told me, he at once killed her and saved her, which made him no less guilty, no less a horrible person.

Reading Dallas's obit on Facebook years later, I imagined his manifold soul above his slumped torso seizured to stillness on the couch, the cloud pouring from his mouth, failing this time to jump-start his own heart.

But when Dallas had told me all this, I figured it must have been a drug-induced hallucination. I mean, we'd all OD'd to greater or lesser degrees. We'd all projected astrally on LSD, or sleep-deprived on uppers, seen our own bodies sprawled and useless. But, after his funeral, as my tolerance increased, as I became Rust's primary driver, his right-hand man, I began to notice I too existed in a strange temporality that couldn't be completely blamed on delirium. I oscillated from full to empty, never lingering in between. I'd pull into Rust's lot with my pockets bulging and shout over the sound of him welding chassis to reified beaters as he readied another jalopy for the next Florida run, and then I'd blink and be pill-less once again, in the same spot, impatient to hit the road. Then all the dope boys became interchangeable. I'd be driving to Florida with S. and W., and then, looking in the rearview, I'd find them replaced by R. and L., or Kilo and Litany. Silent and awkward or conked out with placid smiles, everyone served the same purpose. Then the Feds would crack down on Lauderdale and new clinics would crop up in other cities, in Georgia and Mississippi. But it was the same drive, the same need-fueled jut—ten, fifteen, twenty hours down from snow banks to humid warmth, a tentacled mass swapping out one dope boy for another dope boy, one landscape for another landscape. Even the color and the shape of the pills would change. The only constant was that we needed more than we could ever achieve.

At one point I was on M's couch watching Scag and Brando inject themselves, but instead they drew the liquid out of their bodies, removed the needle from their veins, squirted the stuff back into the spoon. There were other situations too where the world worked in reverse.

We began to talk about escape.

∾

I was reminded of one of Stoneman's lectures on Story, when he said that the quotidian sometimes holds more weight than the sensational. He said, You don't need explosions, death, violence. Write a dinner party or a walk home from the bar. But if I was writing a book about the opioid epidemic, all I had was shock, spikes of emotion connected to vague blurs.

I thought about this while I loaded up the vehicle with dope boys in front of Rust's trailer, listening to Rust clang on metal, engines roaring deep in the field that was Rust's Recks. The sounds were echoes of when that original tornado touched down. We were all waiting for a tornado. We all waited for something to move us, an act of god, prophecy, a palm full of tablets crushed and snorted, a few Speedway gas cards, a set of scrapped-together wheels. All those years as we pushed our luck, jetting off for brief glimpses of southern sunlight, Rust stayed beneath Ohio's cloudy skies. He waited, pounded, and welded new transports for us, planned for a more expeditious getaway.

Rust was our benefactor, our mentor and guide. He'd been using opioid analogues since before Big Pharma called pain the sixth vital sign. When we returned from our trips, we'd sit around his coffee table to split our bounty, count our take, then we'd gather our individual doses and ingest. We all leaned back into the rush, the drip, the numb. I would feel awake again and everything would freeze. I'd watch the room smoke and plume, jellyfish tendrils pouring out of all of us to scatter and reconvene. A mutual loving soul.

Then one day there was Judy, Dallas's bereaved. She stood in the kitchen wearing skintight Cracker Barrel slacks under an apron, her bare arms plump. She blamed us for Dallas's death. I struggled up from the couch, managed my way across the floor where she slapped and scratched at me till I was close enough to hold her. The noise she made sent our blooms scrabbling back into our individual chests, reanimated all of our limbs and torsos, hearts pounding, throats gasping for answers.

She said, It's all your fault. Which we had already accepted into that agglomerate guilt buried deep inside persistent dread. I'd added Dallas's death to the disconnect from my parents, my grandfather's funeral that I skipped, my wasted education, the slim hope of my book. We nodded along with Judy's swell and bellow. She sobbed only briefly. She said, I need to understand why he'd go so far. You owe me. Which we did.

A few pills from each of us as penance, and Judy was hooked. Her own bloom rushed a circle around the room the color of pale green ocean before it charged ours and integrated. She alternately watched our souls and nodded next to me in the low spot of the couch, thigh against thigh in a way that in a more sober era would have been seductive.

◞

It was Judy's idea. She'd learned on the Discovery channel that people all over the US were building rocket ships in which they could escape the earth for some lunar commune where there was no poverty, no ongoing war, where they'd already built a bubble to filter oxygen. Rust took over the operation, employed us to scavenge sheet metal from crumpled Buicks, to swipe bolts and piping from Menards. Judy downloaded the specs from a message board. There were blueprints for the weaponry necessary to protect us from intergalactic invaders, but I think, despite our blooms, we were all doubtful that this alien life could exist, much less mean us harm. I was unsure when Judy leaned her head on my shoulder during yet another Florida trip, somewhere between Nashville and Birmingham. The guilt and want ground around the void between my empty and full. I said, Judy, wake up. Tell me a story or I'm gonna pass out. Everyone else was sleeping and there was little energy left to keep me awake. She blinked, slapped her face, and reached for my zipper.

And I wanted to put all of this on paper, the darkness and the fumble of sex, a quest narrative with a holy pill-mill grail. Judy was my maiden in distress now saved. We worked on the rocket ship all day. We slept on Rust's guest room couch and writhed into each other in a shared sleeping bag. She gained weight off our diet of communal pizzas and Mountain Dew, but I stayed scrawny. I liked the feel of her soft belly as I wrapped an arm around her, holding her flesh so it wouldn't slide off the cushion, hands too busy to even scribble a letter.

✍

Time passed or it didn't. This all occurred over a series of
what? Five years? Less? And once it fell to pieces, I never saw
any of them ever again. So, in a way, I'm younger than my birth
certificate says.

At one point Rench ran off to rehab and later Scag got
nabbed slinging weed. The rocket ship took form, and I banged
a maroon quarter panel to a conical tip while Rust lazed on
his lawn chair. He was shirtless, cave-chested. He plotted. He
said he needed pictures of the clinic next time we took a southbound trip. He wanted to know where security cameras were
positioned, the locations of personnel, guards, receptionists.
He gave me a digital camera to snap the shots. He said, We hit
this lick and it's like a hundred thousand pills, man. You come
straight back here and we blast off and there ain't no laws on the
moon. This was Ohio, fall, leaves scraping across gravel, squir-
rels scurrying to shelter with the racket of much larger beasts.
Judy brought us lunch while we worked. We ate the room-temp
pizza off torn corners of the greasy box. Judy crushed her pills
on a detached rearview mirror, and I noticed she was up to
three at once, ninety milligrams of Roxy required for a buzz. I
was annoyed. I said, What's the fucking point? We're just gonna
run out again. I wanted to tell them I knew the rocket would
never make it, that we were only building to build, soldering
metal to metal for the sake of shattering the static.

Rust gave me a look both wild and anxious, a fury in his
eyes. He said, Something's gonna happen. And then leaned
over to vomit, a noiseless splurge into the dirt yard, and he
came up laughing, tossed me the bottle of pills, an answer or at
least the end of the question.

We loaded into a dinged-up Impala, Judy and me in front,
Rench and Butler in the back, Litany in the middle. Judy

smithereened her tablets, took the fattest line first. Then she passed around the jewel case. She chased the drugs with my Mountain Dew, turned up *Tha Carter II* as I idled at rest stops, ate Snickers and peanuts and left the car in cruise. Day showed us distant foggy mountains and night revealed only headlights, exit signs. We slept in the Walmart parking lot to save hotel funds. Or rather we tried to sleep, but I stayed awake while jellyfish tendrils swarmed about their bodies, dipped in and out of the cracked windows, giving and taking away. I sat on the curb weighted by humidity, then opened up my diminished stash, crushed, inhaled. The pills that remained rattled lonely. I counted and came up short until sunrise, when Butler the phlebotomist took his works into a stall and vanished for good.

～

We returned from Georgia a man short and I handed over an empty camera, no data for a bigger hit. We split our pills and dosed up and then I went on a drive alone for once, windows down and AC on. I took the country roads that Dallas and I used to roadie on, sucked down joint after careless joint.

When I found him in the Walmart bathroom, Butler's hand dangled to the ground, and jellies flashed as I peed until the flashes stopped. That's when I was certain. I'd counted the cameras while I power walked through the sliding doors without him. Seventeen lenses preserved my solitary escape, our car fleeing that Georgia Walmart parking lot, photoless, Butlerless, failed. The questions that Judy and Kilo and Litany posed floated with our blooms, obscured my view all the way to the clinic and beyond, clouded the twelve-hour drive back to Hillbilly Oz and Rust's Recks.

It was only a matter of time before we were caught. We'd all been so set on American Gangstering our trip to riches that we'd missed the fact that life had swiped us by. I took the county highway to the interstate and for the first time in forever I cried over everything that had ended. Then I pulled over to the shoulder and did more pills. I headed back to work on the capsule, anything that would propel us far from earth.

When I pulled in the drive, Litany was painting the scavenged decklid armor with anime characters and graffitied empowerments—*thrive, hope, love.* I complimented her on the art, the colors, the way the blue dripped weirdly on the slick surface, but I also noted that it would all burn off once the capsule broke the atmosphere to which she said, I'm not stupid. I know we aren't going anywhere. It will blow apart before it breaks the ozone layer.

The crooked cone I'd banged out of rusted metal tapered down into a pod outfitted with dirty pilot seats sewn with extra belts and buckles. It weighed over a ton which was actually quite light considering its size, the components used. Along with her favorite heroes and positive words, Litany dedicated an entire panel to a jellyfish bloom, the mutual life force prepared to shock the dead back into being. In her painting, the bloom emerged from a pile of pills to alter time and space, to make room for flying saucers. And seeing those pills, their possibilities, I realized there is no knowing the truth until we try it, and once we've tried the truth it becomes malleable. Altered.

As we prepped the tanks, checked the hoses, I thought of the moment of flight. I imagined how Judy would take my hand while we counted down: Ten. Nine. Eight. At five I would snort a couple pills from a busted shard of glass. We would all snort, inject, smoke. We would need to be in the right headspace for this to work, to get high enough, as in up into the sky, to float in communion with Kilo, our lone and intrepid test pilot. I imagined Judy's large hand, how it would crush mine as she'd make a fist around my fingers while working up a vein. How she'd plunge the needle in, shoot four pills at once. We would all have upped our tolerances, pushing for the perfect high. Then back to the countdown: Three! Two! One! And there would be a sputter, a combustion too soon stifled. The bloom would pour out, surround the ship, an electric storm of our jellyfish lightning, tentacles stinging the craft into a rumble then a hum. It would all happen like magic, and we'd applaud as the capsule rose, fire shooting from every rocket, grass roasted to char. We'd have to back up. It would be marvelous, the spacecraft rising, Kilo rising, the jellyfish bloom rising all as one. And the chains would begin to snap from the ground and as we rushed to grab them, to secure the vessel, we would also lift upward, rise from the earth. And all of that need, all that desire, would leave us with the heave of the rocket ship which would be the result of our own drive to vanish in the firmament. People talk about the search for meaning, of higher powers and ascension, but have they ever felt it? We would feel it. We would leave like Dallas and Butler and Brando and Scag and all the others. It would be wonderful, will be wonderful, to grip the chain in one hand, Judy's fist in the other, and blast off into the sky.

Lifers, Locals, Hangers-on

Once again, Lissa found herself at a party, tipsy, playing therapist to her best friend. Apparently, Glory's most recent ex, a younger guy and a senior in the BFA, had tried to teach her about line breaks—imagine that! *Glory!* the most prolific poet Westinghouse, Ohio had ever known! The two women sat squished together in the dip of the thrifted couch, faded floral stitching merged with wine stains under their asses. Another Literati House party. Another cohort meet-and-greet for the budding creatives who didn't have the scratch to make it on one of the coasts. Every fresh batch of students employed the same excuse: it was cheap here, lowbrow, DIY. As if they were better than middle America, but conceded to condescend. What they didn't realize was that the Midwest was fine without them. Glory was on one: If you've got such a hard-on for traditional forms, then go publish in *Poetry Magazine* like the other stuck-up White dudes. I'm too old and Black for that shit. I'm here to innovate. I want to feel.

Lissa told her friend, Hell yeah! and, Right! and nodded for emphasis, but half her attention was fly-papered to the cowboy in the corner, boot propped against the wall and bolo dangling when he leaned in and pecked at his drink. She watched the dreamy youngsters clique around him and separate, the girls flirt and the boys pretend not to be too drunk. With his worn hat and slumped form, the cowboy stood out. He was early thirties, same age as herself and Glory. A misfit. Lissa let Glory carry on but her mind was on the man in flannel.

Also, misfit wasn't accurate. She and Glory fit in too well. They were lifers, locals, hangers-on. While most of the students were dropped off at the Westinghouse Institute by their parents only to leave four years later, restless and confused, Lissa and Glory were born-and-raised and only grew more comfortable with the community they helped create. Both she and Glory stayed around after undergrad because Westinghouse was the type of small town where idealists like themselves could afford not to make it. They obtained marginal publishing creds and were invited to readings and author events statewide. They had roomed together in Literati House during its foundational years, championed the first noise complaint and christened the carpet with the initial slosh of beer. That was back when it was nothing more than a rental with an absentee landlord and plumbing problems. Now they owned the place outright, an artspace and gallery. A nonprofit haltered only by restricted funds and a community whose support centered around the public pool, with arts shoved to the periphery. Literati House hosted parties and experimental shows, screened films about absolutely nothing. The first-year party was a rite of passage for the creatives of Westinghouse Institute, a welcome to a community they would invest in for four years and then most likely forget.

Glory was silent which meant Lissa owed her an answer, but Lissa had nothing. Glory repeated herself, I said what's up with John Wayne? She nodded at the stud in the corner.

Um, said Lissa.

You've been ogling him all night.

Now it was Glory's turn to be the analyst. She asked Lissa if her attraction to the cowboy signaled a repressed desire to ride out West, and she meant, *ride*. She asked if this cowboy fetish could actually be Lissa's innate desire to lasso and hogtie, like maybe she was turned on by that.

It was too much. Lissa blushed and laughed like none of what her friend said was true. He was odd, that's all. He didn't fit into this scene. She laughed because she'd been thinking recently about the West as a concept, not a place. The West, to Lissa, signaled both escape and self-discovery. Besides Manifest Destiny or the ravaging of the natural world for money, the West was a consideration of breaking life down to its survival basics and from there distinguishing good and bad. She'd begun to crave this simple binary of life ever since Tom stopped drinking and going out. He was preparing for grad school, applying to online degrees and universities close enough to commute, so they wouldn't have to move or anything. It shouldn't be that big of a deal. Though his newfound focus was inherently good, the arrangement felt stifling. She didn't want to leave, but now was stuck. They'd been together five years and cohosted a hundred gatherings, but now she had to party alone while he stayed in. Once upon a time they'd taken edibles and shared a hip flask through a drive-in movie, but now he called movies *films* and *studied* instead of read. It wasn't the West as a physical space that she considered, but the simplicity of it, the myth of black hats and white hats, of how to distinguish right and wrong. She also longed for its wildness.

The Cowboy in the corner wore a hat with a grayish morality, but it had once been brown. He also wasn't in the corner anymore. Hands wedged into his pockets and a Marlboro in his mouth, he hove through the door.

Glory never liked Tom anyway. She said, Go, girl. Follow him. Yeehaw!

It wasn't like Tom was waiting up.

As Lissa broke beyond the billow-haze of blunt smoke on the porch, she saw the Cowboy sitting on the steps alone. He flipped a pistol from his side, no longer than his forefinger and flicked out a small, wavering flame. He lit up and the smoke curled through his mustache, around his hat brim. Lissa hopped down in front of him, held her finger guns at her hips, legs saddle-width apart. She stepped a few paces back and said, Draw!

He was slow and Lissa gunned him down, slumped his body into the porch where he made hand motions of effusive blood loss. When he was done dying she said, Howdy. I'm Lissa.

He stretched out his hand and said his name.

∽

Lissa told Tom she'd be back at nine, but she was an hour late and he was halfway through his film. He dropped his pen to put his arm around her when she slumped into her spot and paused the film to catch her up. *El Topo*, he said, and he gave her a brief history of the Acid Western genre.

Lissa was buzzkilled. Guilty. Tom splayed Lissa's cowboy crush wide and deconstructed the West till it was warped and disgusting. She watched as the cowboy on the screen introduced a naked child to the psychedelic terrors of the world. A black hat, a gunslinger. Her world was all wrong and Tom was calling her out.

Tom went to bed when the credits rolled, but Lissa hit her weed pen on the couch to calm down. She'd been with Tom ever since the night five years ago when she carded him on his twenty-first birthday. In the intervening years, no matter how often the G&T Bar patrons flirted or passed her their number, Lissa never considered a change to the pattern and flow of their lives. In the daytime she worked on her novel-in-progress in which the main characters were caring partners. She wanted to break the literary tradition of strained affairs, but the corral around her lovers' hearts kept breaking open, the gate kept getting sprung.

She thought about the Cowboy who was also a writer, straight out of his MFA and adjuncting at the Institute. As they sat side-by-side on the Literati House steps, he had asked if they could exchange numbers under the pretense of future collaboration and community. Now, a bit loopy on the couch, Lissa started a new message, deleted it.

∽

The question wasn't about being faithful. It was: should I stay or should I go?

The Clash hashed out their query over the G&T Bar jukebox and Lissa thought *Fuck off! Too on the nose.*

She rarely had customers, but the owner was rich and didn't care. He started this establishment in the sixties and didn't want his legacy glitzed up by hip MBAs in the name of revitalization or progress, so the dank decor never changed. Zeppelin and Pink Floyd posters papered the ceiling and 69s and peace signs cut into the bar. On dead nights, Glory kept her company while she worked. Over scotch rocks in the empty bar, Lissa explained to Glory that it wasn't a crush and that it wasn't wrong to want what you couldn't have as long as you didn't structure your world around what was missing. She said, I love Tom. But he's sort of selfish and boring right now.

Glory hmmmphed and swiped left on her phone.

Lissa said, What?

Glory looked at her: So you just stay with Tom the rest of your life? Bartend. Write. What?

Lissa said, I mean. It's worked so far.

Boring, selfish Tom?

Glory was getting drunk, poetic, profound. When she was faded, she tended to point her finger and pontificate. She said, Come on, babe! Tom's boring. Love's not worth a shit unless it makes us want to fuck, fly, and sing!

I never said he was boring, Lissa said. But she realized that's exactly the word she'd used. Boring. Selfish. Not just Tom. Everything.

Glory slammed her phone on the bar and the women let the gavel-clap echo. They'd never talked about moving on or about Literati House as anything but a permanent institution, but in the dust mote spotlights of the G&T Bar on this Tuesday night, the image of Westinghouse, Ohio darkened, smudged. Glory broke the veil: Everything here, we built it on our own. And the Foundation just wants *results*? The classes we teach have to *result* in *jobs*?

Lissa said, They'll pull our funding?

Not just that, said Glory. This whole writing life. We fight to prove our relevance while this town, this world, just turns the page, changes the subject. We could live anywhere, babe.

Lissa felt the booze. She said, We could kick New York's ass.

Damn right! We could go anywhere! Glory cooled. I mean, I got my folks here, but, metaphorically.

The door creaked open, slammed shut. Lissa squinted, too short of desire to pretend she was on the clock. Hello? she said.

Howdy. The voice came from an unmistakable sauntering form, capped with his Stetson. I heard shouting, the Cowboy said.

She must have mentioned where she worked. It was a small town. She shouldn't be surprised. She was calm, cool, and affected a drawl: What brings you around these parts, pardner?

He leaned his hip into the bar next to Lissa.

Well, he said, I met a local gal the other night who said this was the best watering hole east of the Mississippi.

Glory hmmmphed.

Lissa gave her an evil eye.

The Cowboy said, Don't mean to interrupt.

No worries. Lissa rounded to her side of the bar. She said, Where'd you hitch your horse?

Mitch laughed and dropped his drawl to let her know that ranching wasn't what it used to be. They used ATVs these days, slept beyond sunrise. Everything had changed with the invention of barbed wire. Lots of people didn't wear denim. Smoke? he asked her. But Glory leaned over and snatched the cigarette from his hand, had the Marlboro lit before he'd finished word one. He said, It's just a get-up, an identity thing. He opened his hands and waved them down his own wardrobe. Feels cozy. I like it.

Glory exhaled: We do too, Cowboy.

Everyone blushed.

Over whiskeys, Mitch told the women about his years on the range. Montana. Star-splurged nights. Magic. Kerouac came through at one time or another and scrawled a poem on his granddad's barn where he spent the night. A scribble about coyotes in the panoply of night terrors. Not famous, but quiet. Chill. A town where the post office is also the general store and the only bar for thirty miles. Lonely, he said, But the good kind of lonely. I'd write stories and poems and read them aloud in the wilderness knowing no one would ever hear me. He told them about bar fights and snake bites and banging sticks together to fend off a bear. His America was another mythical world. An open world, free of iPhones and internet: society's modern constraints. He talked about going off to college and being a loner and missing his stool at the tavern, bone-tired and surrounded by quiet brooding saddle-sore men.

It sounded beautiful. Lissa wanted to be lonely and stoic, speak little, each word flush with meaning, but when the regulars began to trickle in, she poured their PBRs and slid them their saltshakers and collected their twenties until she sobered up. She traded working class banter with retired steelworkers and cubical speak with the call center's second shift. Glory called a friend for a ride and when Lissa remembered to check on the Cowboy, he'd vanished, not a trace but his whiskey killed and upside-down glass, a note scrawled on a napkin: *See you in the wild blue yonder, pard.*

⌒

When Lissa woke at the tail end of morning, her life hadn't changed. Weeks went by and when she stumbled into the kitchen, the coffee pot was already half empty and Tom was fully submerged in an ocean of tomes. Texts, not books.

She sat at the dining room table and typed words into her novel, but she couldn't decide what to make her protagonist want. The fictional couple was supposed to be huddled in their basement bathtub while tornado sirens blared in the distance, but the woman kept going out to check on things: her handmade quilt, some cans of soup, her car. There was no doubt about it: Lissa's inner world was in foment. The woman was in her car, driving the hell away. Lissa jumped when Tom reached over her shoulder to refill her coffee and kiss her on the cheek. Coffee sloshed onto the table and pooled by her laptop, but she didn't clean it up or move away. Tom asked, What's up? But she didn't have the answer, only a question.

She caught Tom's arm, Have you thought about applying anywhere outside of Ohio?

He squinted at her, silent, coffee pot in his hand. He'd moved to Westinghouse from Connecticut and only went back to visit over holidays. Lissa's folks were long lost to a galaxy of drugs, and her foster parents had followed their church to Michigan, so there wasn't anything to tie her here.

But Ohio is our home, he said. We love it here.

What if it was a dream school? Lots of fellowships and stuff?

Well, he said, No. I don't know.

Lissa said, What if it's an adventure, just to see. But Tom looked confused. She said, The point is that we don't know about anywhere cause we haven't looked.

It was his turn for questions: Are you unhappy? What's wrong?

Lissa returned to her MacBook and its baffled protagonists. Originally she wanted them to live in a bubble but the world kept intruding. The world changed. It invaded and brought unasked-for questions that altered their lives.

Tom said, What's up, babe? Anything I can do?

Nothing, she said. Never mind. It's just the novel. Blah.

∽

When the leaves turned and they both had a Monday off, Glory showed up at Lissa's front door with a bag of Holy Blue Caps and they ate the mushrooms blended with peanut butter over toast. Glory drove and Lissa watched her world of Westinghouse, Ohio change from its historic brick buildings and shops to the grown-over trailers of the extant cult to the wilderness of the state park. With the top down and the sun jacket-warm, Lissa could see the lines of air as they ramped over the windshield and flicked fingers through her hair.

The overlook parking lot was empty when they arrived, so

they spread a blanket alone on the edge of a vast gully carved a bajillion years ago by glaciers. Lissa watched the vultures arc at eye level. Somewhere, an eagle screamed. She imagined the Cowboy in situations she didn't want to think about but still wanted. She in her sundress and his rough Cowboy fingers playing with the hem. Her body buzzed from the mushrooms and lust, even though she was all alone.

But the Cowboy *was* there, behind her and Glory, announcing his howdy into the gaping world. As another Blue Cap wave washed over her, the Cowboy guided the trip to a specific patch of foliage aflame or a squirrel who sat on its haunches to watch them. He fired off his gun, one cigarette after another, the noise rippling through her body, rush and tingle. Glory sat behind Lissa and played with her hair. She whispered poetry from memory into Lissa's ear, idylls and odes, her voice the calm hum of true meaning. At a point of singular energy, they all stood and sounded their yawps into the valley, and the valley hooted back. When the sun clopped off behind the far ridge, the Cowboy built a small fire and heated beans which they scooped from a can with its bent lid.

By sunset, Lissa's giddiness was gone and she wondered aloud how the Cowboy had scored a day off teaching. How had he known to come here?

He laughed and leaned back on the blanket, pointed to the pinkish line on the horizon, and said, Isn't this more important than school? Isn't this better than reading or writing or answering questions?

Lissa admitted he was right.

Her final question was how did he get there, but it seemed intrusive to ask. Glory had to host a reading and Lissa was supposed to relieve Dunk at seven, so they chugged water and packed up their blanket before they realized the Cowboy didn't have a car. On the return trip to Westinghouse, he rode with them in Glory's drop-top, his feet propped on the back seat, sharing the cool wind with them, while the world flashed by.

⌒

The leaves fell and autumn cooled. It was strange that Lissa didn't see the Cowboy more often. In a town this small, people were omnipresent: at the coffee shop, at the bar, walking down the sidewalk and waving like it was *Sesame Street*.

Nights off, she watched Tom's films: *Zachariah, Dead Man, Blueberry*, all hints that he was clued in to her wanderlust, her cheating life. In the mornings she critiqued his letters of application, and in the evenings she grew bored, listless. When they shared scotches at the G&T, Lissa drifted away from Glory's tales of trysts with horny young men, slipped through a crack in the door two thousand miles away where she galloped along sandstone gorges to the lonely hoot of a train. While hanging the new show at Literati House, Lissa found herself uninterested in the abstract sprawl of amateur art. All this beautiful, difficult work for a couple dozen viewers who dropped a dollar or two in the donation bucket, who stopped by briefly when they had free time, but often had more important things to do. She strung up the pieces out of sequence, the timeline skewed, so that they presented as constant sunset rather than the progression of darkness to flame that the artist preferred.

Of course Glory noticed. She said, What the fuck's the matter?

But Lissa didn't know. Nothing she once held dear had changed. It was all perfectly, stupidly the same.

That night, the regulars came into the G&T for their after-supper nightcaps. Nicky and Mickey, retired mechanics who packed their days with project cars. She clunked their respective mugs in front of them and changed their twenties for a stack of bills and quarters. The night slogged on with the usual quiet exchanges, cars and parts and prices. On his third drink, Mickey slipped her a one and when she gripped the bill, he held on to his end. She tugged half-heartedly. Sighed. Gave up.

He said, Gotta get my smile first.

Obnoxious, but nothing new. Most of her adult life she'd handled their banter. She said, I can't help but smile at your ugly ass.

They all three laughed, but Mickey held on.

Really honey, he said, If I were about thirty years younger.

Nicky said, Come on, Mick. And clapped his friend on the back.

Just saying, said Mickey.

Same as any other night, the quips and ribbing. Just a bit more tedious. The jokes were all seventy years old and flaccid. She snatched her dollar and called them bastards, fake hurt, and Mickey and Nicky cracked wise back until a shadow fell over them.

The Cowboy said, Is there a problem?

His hands were in his pockets, but he removed one to brush back his jacket and reveal the pistol holstered at his waist. Bigger than a finger gun with a battle-worn grip and a glint on the shined barrel.

Well shit, said Nicky, We got ourselves a real rootin' tootin' one here, Mick.

Mick said, We're just joshing.

The Cowboy wasn't satisfied. His hand fell to just inches above the grip. You bothering this woman?

Lissa tried to tell him you can't expect old Westinghouse retirees to change, but she blushed instead. She gaped. It was all too real.

Both Nicky and Mickey stuck their hands in the air like a hold-up.

The Cowboy said, Is it fine? He said, Where I come from there's a thing called respect and a thing called justice and it ain't fine if either one of them's missing.

She opened her mouth, but couldn't find the words. No. It wasn't fine, not really. None of it was fine at all anymore. She was sick of it.

Nicky said, Never mind. We was just leaving.

Mickey gulped beer and scraped up off his stool. Yeah, just heading out.

As the Cowboy ushered them through the door, a part of Lissa wanted to stop him. A gunfight, really? Taking them outside? But the rest of her wanted to follow and watch the action go down, to clap her hands as the Cowboy drew first and afterward she'd swing onto the back of his horse and ride west with him till the ocean blocked their way.

Instead, the door closed behind them and she was alone. The jukebox played Waylon Jennings like it was in on the plan, but Waylon crooned a sad song, a lonely song, a song that yearned for a moment of peace. As she cleared the glasses and wiped down the counter, she wondered what she would do tomorrow, next week, when Nick and Mickey either showed back up or didn't. Life could've gone on the same without the Cowboy's appearance in town. Now everything had to change.

When Lissa shut off the lights and stepped outside, she was surprised that the city had become a snowy ghost town, not a tire track on the dusted street. She locked the door and stared off in the direction of the retired mill, just smokestacks on the horizon and in the other direction, West, not so much a destination as an open space. There was an object in the road, a dark mound, and she walked toward the piece of trash, walked west toward the Cowboy's hat, snowless, not even wet. She flipped it up onto her head and the fit was perfect. She said, Howdy, and her voice wasn't faint and wobbly but gruff like tractor tires cutting up gravel. Howdy, she said to the wild white yonder.

She held her hands at her hips. Simple as that. Thumbs cocked, ready to begin.

Psychedelicious

By the time Allen fired up the grill at the Great Midwest Beer Fest, we were already food truck experts, smash burger virtuosos, burrito hotshots, savants of kimchi slaw. When I glanced out the service window, the crooked queue of beer enthusiasts stretched beyond the kegerator tents, proving *Psychedelicious Street Food's* weird allure. Allen told me, Who doesn't like beer and greasy grub? What could go wrong? A culmination of his batshit dreams and our grueling effort, of nights where Allen killed his beer and hit the hay, leaving me to soak and scrub the dishes alone. This was success, and we shared the pride between us. What could go wrong, I wondered, when Allen always won? A question I, the loser, could not properly ponder.

We traded food for sample pours from Dad Bod Beer, the festival's host, their brews named things like Double Dry-Hopped Terpene Dream. Live bands droned from the stage in the meadow and heads swarmed with woozy vibes. I told the customers it was a twenty-minute wait. Twenty-five. Thirty. Allen said: Catch up. I mangled a name barely audible above

the psych rock background din and passed the paper tray to
the appropriate hungry hands. My mouth was dry, so I tipped
the last sip of beer foam and felt wings fumble around my
mouth before the stinger pierced my tongue. I screamed and
the wasp missiled out, undamaged. The taco tray hit the ceiling
and I lurched into Allen. His palm sizzled on the grill. We
spun, tumbled, collided, the space too tight to dance out of one
another's way.

He said, What the fuck?

I said, Mfhfmblfth.

The swinging slapbox of Allen's hands. The dodge and
mumble of my swelling face.

෴

The plan for the summer was to stuff myself in a space too
hot, too cramped to think. A relief. My philosophy was that
if I kept busy I could clear my head, but my thoughts continued to reel. I'd been listless since April, before I defended my
thesis and graduated with a master's and a mountain of debt.
PhD rejections piled on and my partner, Callie, signed up for
a doctorate out West, said we should take time to ourselves. I
was hesitant and lacked focus. I broke my lease, drove the six
hours from DC to Ohio, and took up residence with the wolf
spiders in my parents' basement. Academia was a ladder, but
what happens when you run out of rungs? The answer: I laid in
bed for a week. No clear direction, no definite point. I'd put so
much effort into drawing a line between my promising future
and my more troublesome past. New number, no social media,
a jumble of addresses without forwarded mail. I'd never considered my mom handing me the cordless, another relic. I didn't
expect Allen's voice in the receiver, my best friend from a life
forgotten. I answered with a frown. He said, Welcome home,

Billy Boy! Good timing. I had a dream!

I sat up. Riveted. I said, What?

He said, Listen. We gotta act fast. Come by.

Sure, I said. I had nothing better to do.

We formulated a plan. Two days later, he pulled out the Hide-A-Bed in his spare room and offered me a place to stay.

Allen said he was better now, a changed man. A few drinks per day and a bit of pot. He looked clean. This fresh incarnation with his tight haircut and button-down, long sleeves that sheathed his stick-and-pokes. He'd lost two fingers since I last saw him. I noticed when he held up the envelope of food truck seed cash. He explained: Outback Steakhouse meat slicer. Grease-slicked floors. A wake-up call. A boost forward. A cash settlement. He shook the envelope, fingerless, in my face.

I backed my car out of the drive and he explained his success. He said, I listened to this podcast. All about putting your plan out there. Speak it. Write it. The universe will respond. He said that the plan for the food truck came to him while he slept, the night before the meat slicer accident proved it a reality. Luck. Fate. All you had to do was pay attention, keep your eyes peeled for a sign.

Hokey, I said. I didn't want to be a dick, just reasonable. I rebutted that it wasn't that way for all of us. I said some people work hard all their lives and never get an answer.

He said, It's not about you. Don't force it. The universe is saying something right now. Roll down your window. Take a hit. Breathe in the air.

He reached his vaporizer toward me, but I waved it away. Clean for seven years at that point except the occasional drink. All I saw was sunshine, the sprigs of knee-high corn, the wind's judder through the cab. I merged from farmland into downtown Westinghouse, Ohio: Derelict banks and offices, the boarded up Worlinger Department Store. The same city, same abandoned buildings I'd explored with Allen back when we were delinquents, drug heads. The same bent signpost where we'd practiced boardslides and the rooftops where we'd star-gaze, stoned, awed by the cosmos. As I took a left onto Main Street, though, I noticed the meters were replaced by a single kiosk. The fire escapes repainted or gone. Westinghouse, a city we knew from brick to rumor, now featured coffee shops, galleries, a microbrewery in the refurbished space that used to be a mortuary. The sign over the beer garden depicted a phoenix emerging from its pile of ash. Renewal. A message too blatant to be mine.

We were supposed to pick up a retired FedEx truck from Hillbilly Oz, a neglected company town once hailed as the *heart of the opioid epidemic.* At the time it was a thrill to be at the throbbing center of anything at all, but as I entered the old park, I looked down at the trap homes from my eco-friendly ivory tower and my stomach turned.

I said, You promise no drugs, right?

I cornered past one old dealer's house, spinners on a Caddy parked in the dirt yard.

He shook his head. I told you, man. I've changed. We all have.

The road broke down to gravel, signs that threatened Beware of Dog and Trespassers Will Be Shot, the words Rusts Recks spray-painted onto plywood without the apostrophe or the W. Pit bulls paced my Prius. Familiar hope and dread. I was tickled with the hot-blood promise of fresh painkillers, giddy with the rekindled fire of expectation that's adjacent to the high itself. I barked the tires and shook my head to clear out the past, but it lingered, nostalgia and trauma in the same dose. The dogs squatted, straight-edge teens in between songs, panting, ready at any moment to mosh.

Allen was telling the truth: Rust wasn't any longer the scrawny pit-eyed thug who'd funded carpools to Florida pill mills. He banged out of his trailer to meet us, belly slung up in a tucked-in tank top stained with Doritos crumbs. When we hugged, he slapped the wind from my lungs, but there was comfort in his hairy arms, his greeting: Missed you, bub. There was comfort in the lazy way he recounted the peaks and valleys of his career: his drug ring busted, followed by a battle to scrape by above the board. He said, When Allen told me about this investment, I figured a second venture couldn't hurt.

We passed a row of dismantled Jeeps, not enough parts between them to piece together a full Wrangler.

I said, Investment? Venture? I turned to Allen for an explanation, but Allen changed the subject. He said, Look at us! Business owners. Who would've known?

The vehicle heaped in a lonely spot of yard. A box truck in all its mud-smeared glory. It was as Rust described it: a fixer-upper with a wasp problem. One hell of a deal.

He handed us each a can of RAID and we braced ourselves. The mad buzz rushed my ears as Rust rolled up the door. We opened fire.

༄

My summer dove into a muggy Midwest slog, but I took the oppressive heat as my penance, learned to see the sweat of my brow as liberation. Our schedule was packed with visits to farmers and butchers, buying organic, local, and in bulk. Our fingers ached throughout days of dicing, adjusting recipes and prep time. Our fare skewed toward adventurous palates, multicultural delicacies blended with working-class American flare. Allen had the idea to add alcohol to every dish, so there was a shot of mezcal in our guacamole and local rice lager toned the bulgogi marinade, a quirk, a niche. We sampled, wordless. Nodded or shook our heads. Weird. Delicious. Fresh. Other days I scoured crannies of the truck for secret wasp nests while Allen Sawzalled windows into the walls. We followed YouTube tutorials on electric and gas, bolted coolers to the floor. When it came time to sandblast the exterior, we rented the machine and blew through the layers to the original dull shine. Blank space. Stripped down to nothing, it was easy to rebuild.

Despite my better judgment, Allen tripped mushrooms and we jammed the Flaming Lips, went wild with the paint. He said he'd be fine. A couple caps, not a spiral. Inspiration, he explained, as the name *Psychedelicious* bloomed large along the paneling, psychotropic splashes of color against black rims and bumpers. Mistakes turned freeform sprawl, unrestricted, wild.

Allen said, Pretty good for an art school dropout, yeah?

And I had to agree. I stepped back, took it in. Impressive. A business to be proud of. Our own.

A drum solo beat arrhythmically at the fog that late May morning. *Angels and Demons at Play*. When the paint hardened, we parked the truck in the driveway for all to see and shuttled serving trays to the front yard: pulled pork sliders with kimchi slaw, tacos with chicken, bacon, ranch. At first I argued about regulations, inspections, licenses to serve, but I gave in when the money began to flow. Day two, we backed up traffic for a block. We passed fries to the nurses of Westinghouse General, dipped cups of pickle potato salad for shift change cops. Day three, overwhelmed, Allen talked me into taking a hit from his weed pen on a trip between the folding table and the grill. One tiny puff, for medicinal reasons, a celebratory buzz, and as I wadded patties and pressed them into the grill, I popped each bubble of worry that floated through my head. We tipped the health inspector with cupcakes. The mayor tweeted our photo: Westinghouse's own!

The day that the truck passed inspection, we walked to the G&T Bar to celebrate. Both of us broke from our investment, but I offered my credit card to start a tab and ordered shots of Patrón. Allen thunked his finger stub gavel on the bar and ordered another shot and I thought about how far we'd come. On our own terms. He added a drink to my tab for the woman beside him. Didn't ask me, but we weren't the type of people obsessed with money. I didn't pay rent. We shared. I said, I got you. As long as we did what we loved. As long as our business scraped by. Another shot and I met the bartender's gaze, aware that I was overdrinking. Drunk. She winked. Another round. A celebration. I met her eyes, then smiled into my beer. A corner turned. Let's try this again.

What? Allen asked. He texted furiously and slammed the phone into the bar.

Her, I said, The bartender with the tattoo.

Allen was back to muttering curses into his phone. I said, Should I tell her I dig the tattoo?

It was a bird on her bicep adorned with a crown and I had an inkling of the folklore it referenced, but I'd forgotten how to flirt. Allen thumped the phone back down. Distracted. Yeah, he said. Hit that shit.

He said, Let's have a smoke. Come on.

He bummed two cigarettes from a couple on the patio and stuck them both in his mouth to light. I didn't smoke anymore, but he waved away my excuses, plugged the Newport into my mouth. For old time's sake. Needles of menthol, fire and ice. My head floated.

I said, About that bartender.

Allen clawed my shoulder. This is serious, he said, If Rust comes around, you need to call the cops.

He held his phone in his right hand, and it lit up with text after text. It was going so well. We'd see profit in a matter of weeks.

Seriously, Billy Boy. He's trying to fuck us.

How? I remembered Rust's words: investment, venture, *our*. I said, You cut corners, yeah? What did you do?

He said, Jesus, dude. You're so uptight.

So, we owe him?

The patio lurched and my stomach barrel-rolled, the booze catching up. I hit the cigarette which drew the heat from belly to head, but only for a moment. Allen said every time he tries, it's like there's something there to fuck him up. Something out there to get him. Everything he does, there's someone who wants to bust his balls. But it was hard for me to listen. My stomach crawled up my throat. I mumbled and wove off to find the bathroom, slipped inside and bolted the door, bowed to the toilet, and all the pressure poured out, each doubt and hesitation purged, flushed away. I stayed there for a time, waiting, sobering, spilling my guts. Someone knocked, but the knocker moved on. I puked again, waited till I was sure I was empty. I couldn't remember the last time I was drunk.

When I returned to the patio, Allen wasn't there. He wasn't at the bar when I sat at my stool and the Deadhead owner returned with my tab. He said my friend had taken off with the other bartender. Inconvenient, he said. Her leaving him alone. A damn shame.

From the parking lot, I saw the sky splurged with stars. So little light pollution, traffic so many miles away that time itself was reduced to a plod. I couldn't any longer claim this town. I had no name here. Little to call my own. It's not like I'd asked out the bartender. I never asked Allen to wait. My fault: I'd been too drunk, too unsure, to act on my desires. Of course she chose Allen, confidence over indecision. It wasn't so awful to wander home alone, too busy, I decided, to bother with falling in love.

ᔕ

The Midwest Beer Fest was in July and *Psychedelicious* scored a coveted invite. Mad respect. Our name was known. It appeared to me that the business was flourishing but Allen grumbled that we weren't making shit.

The morning of the beer fest, he woke up late, but I drove fast and hustled with the setup and we were parked, windows wide, meat on the grill just in time. While I shuffled orders around, he complained about the heat, his headache. He cursed and drank as he shuffled meat around the flattop. All the vibes from the month before had swiveled. This was the old Allen, grubby, angry, bored. I did my best to pick up the slack, to keep the fervor flowing toward our future.

I sipped my beer and was wasp-stung, Allen-smacked. Swollen-tongued, languageless, I stumbled off the truck alone, pitched past the line of hungry zythophiles and Cicerones, past the booths of Malty Mother Brewing and Humble Raccoon. The heady beer humidity carried me to the first aid tent where Lilly, the volunteer nurse, fed me cubes of ice until the swelling went down. She dropped two Ibuprofen in one hand and set an IPA in the other. Take this, she said. You'll survive.

She had purple hair and a gentle touch that fluttered my heart. My tongue was too beefy to speak, so she filled in the next half hour of my silence. The hoppy beer she passed me was West Coast, the only style she drank because the brewing world was oversaturated with hazies. It was a recipe she'd experimented with while at med school and perfected when she was kicked out of the dorms. Now it was the flagship at Dad Bod Beer who hosted the festival each year.

A touch of honey, she said. In your case, it's a bit ironic.

I must have looked confused, because she said, Yes. A woman. A brewer. But part of me used to want to be a nurse.

I nodded, beamed apologies on brain waves from inside my head to hers. I didn't know what to do with my hands, how to respond, but she refilled my fist with a fresh drink and carried on. She pointed at my shirt, the *Psychedelicious* logo, and said she'd heard positive reviews. She said, Heard the owner's an asshole.

I laughed around my tongue, but the swelling was diminished.

She pulled a joint from behind her ear and fired it up, a shrug like, What are they gonna do? Fire me? She explained, No one ever signs up to volunteer at these things. It's generally just me.

I imagined the two of us in the future, my chef to her brewer, at subsequent beer fests, volunteering at the first aid tent, curing hydration with Gatorade, food for those who overpoured and wound up drunk. Beer and Advil for the pain. She offered me the joint and I was too afraid of fucking up all our possibilities to decline. I didn't inhale, though, only swished the smoke and when the taste grew faint, released it.

She said, Come on. You gotta really hit it, and before I could make up my mind to ask her out, she drew deeply and kissed me. College party, shotgun, kid shit, the smoke shared between our open lips. When she pulled away, I coughed. Bubble-worries busted before impact. My tongue loosened and I talked. It all came out. The wasted degrees, the failure. Allen's warnings about Rust. The food truck had been fun, had been magic, but as I sat with Lilly, I realized I didn't want to go back.

But you love it, right? she said.

I nodded, but I wasn't really sure if it was my love or Allen's, if it was the food itself, or the truck itself, or that over the last few years of disappointment I'd outsourced my joy, glued it to other people's plans. Before I went to school, I wanted to be a gangster like Rust and Allen. But that path was untenable for a scrawny confused White boy. Now I was onto something new.

What do you love? she asked as she lifted a finger and guided the cup to my lips, a marriage of Riwaka and Nelson Sauvin hops. My body hovered, divine as her kiss.

Beer! I said, holding up my cup. I was only half joking. I said, I don't know. I used to think I was a writer.

∽

The sun was hot, but not as high as when I'd entered the tent. The air outside wasn't so stuffy as the live music wailed and growled. Voices carried, indistinguishable, and across the lot *Psychedelicious* squatted, lonely, shuttered, without a line. Allen had given up. I crossed the lot and lunged aboard, ready to open the windows and finish out the day, but the flattop was scraped clean, the prep table shut, everything bungeed, resecured. Allen was hitting his hash in the back corner. He said, Fuck this shit. I'm tired. Let's go.

The truck spat gravel as we exited the lot, bouldered onto the open road. The dream was in its death throes. But my phone vibrated in my pocket: Lilly. It would all work out. Each vibration was a ripple in my ever-evolving plan. Allen cornered too hard and the truck tipped, so he slammed on the brakes and we swayed, righted. Fucked up. Restless. Filled with rage. I offered to take the wheel. The least I could do was get us home alive, but Allen thumped his three remaining fingers on the wheel, that confidence reemerging. He said, I'll get your ass there. Trust me.

I didn't. Another sharp curve. Up ahead, the road Y-ed off with a stop sign coming the other direction at which no one ever stopped. The sightline was awful. The place was known for accidents. Allen sped up. He asked how much we'd get from the insurance. Twenty, thirty thousand?

I said, You better fucking not.

I read and reread Lilly's text, a mantra.

More work than it's worth, Allen said. Barely any time to sleep, and for what? We give Rust his cut just to sit around?

Stop.

But he went on. All the problems that money alone could solve. Allen treated words as currency: as if he could throw enough out there to right any wrong. He talked too much and didn't listen to the buzz, too tuned in to his excuses to see the whirlwind of wasps around his head. A nest I must've missed. A swarm.

He punched the headliner, said, Sometimes, you listen to the universe and you think you've heard it right, but you really heard it wrong. Listen harder! He slapped at the insect cloud around his face.

I said, Stop! Pull over.

But Allen wasn't done. He barreled us toward the intersection. He said, I know I haven't been straight with you about all of this, but we'll get our money. We'll make it right.

This was the old Allen.

I said, Stop!

He cursed and slapped. His eyes bulged in recognition. The first sting. He swerved, stomped the brakes, and the truck swayed, implements crashing in the back. We skidded sideways and I saw all of it, a vision of the end.

Years later, Lilly and I would tour the breweries of Virginia together, myself as a reviewer and Lilly as a beer rep. And though we would break off our engagement after half a dozen years of life together, our relationship wouldn't be wasted. Eventually we'd move on and later, Lilly would call me from Westinghouse, Ohio where she now worked as head brewer for a micro specializing in sours. I'd be in Colorado at the time, writing, savoring my beer, and she'd tell me Allen passed away.

No cause listed, only *in the night*, which at just forty-five years of age rings nefarious. And I'd know what I knew all along: That the fervor can't last forever. That you can't make meaning by glomming onto other people's dreams. I would thank Lilly for letting me know. I'd worry that I might cry. But I wouldn't let myself.

Instead, I'd think back on the summer when I started a food truck with my best friend because it made him so happy and because he wanted me there and I didn't know what else to do. I'd think back to the moment when the swarm descended on us, skidding sideways along Ohio backroads, and how I hesitated, afraid to make the jump. Afraid to leave Allen alone. But he shouted another fact about the universe, another platitude or mantra, like if we went with the flow it'd all work out. He said, Trust me. A stupid thing to say. I didn't. I chose. The truck was still careening, but I pulled and the door slid open. I flung my body out.

Orange Pill,
Yellow Wrangler

Mary

I'll tell you about the time I cheated on Mary and she died.

She had this polka dot of a nose I'd kiss before I lifted her hair, before she ducked into a line.

Blinked her blown pupils.

I don't honestly know if she's dead or alive, but after her seizure, not a word, not a text, and somehow it's easier to believe she's gone for good because that way, the guilt can rush me and dissipate, instead of stringing me along.

She used to string me along.

She'd wink at me and walk away.

First time we kissed in high school, Flame Day, where we celebrated sports and mocked humanity, she said, Hold my hand and when I did, her palm shocked me, a jolt. I said, What the fuck? And she held up the buzzer.

We didn't stop searching for that jolt.

Now my calls all go to voicemail.

The mailbox is always full.

I want to tell you I cheated with the Jeep Girl, but she was hardly even real, a figment I floated with for a couple hours' drive before the mirage punctured and farted off.

I want to say it doesn't feel like a lie.

Mary took forever to get ready, so I'd crank Linkin Park in the car and build my irritation into rage and then Mary'd slide in on the passenger side and say, Punch it, Chewie.

Every single time.

Like each day she was born into a different world that loved her and I loved her and the world loved us both.

Until it didn't.

Now I lie in our empty bed.

I call until the battery dies.

The Jeep Girl

Twenty miles from the Suboxone clinic in Toledo and Mary's zonked open-mouthed beside me and she lets out a Wookiee snore and I'm like *goddamn asshole* to the yellow Wrangler all up on my tail and I'm like *three open lanes* because I-75 just gapes in front of us nothing anywhere around but Mary doesn't care and I think *wake up* and say *look at this shit* but nothing not a stir so I brake-check the bitch behind me which makes Mary's slumped head nod and I crank down the window to give the driver an undeniable middle finger like *look at this fuck you fuck you fuck you* when the Jeep pulls alongside and matches my speed and I see this woman wave at me and she's a hurricane of hair in a low-cut bloom of supermodel boobs and I see her Miss Ohio smile before she blows me a fucking kiss and takes the exit but now I float off to another plane where I listen to her whisper the kind of low talk after sex those words between only us and god like *I love you* and *I want you* and *that was fucking good* and we have this house by the lake and it's Tom Petty rocking in the Wrangler and we innocently hold hands and neck and in this daydream I get my kicks motoring a lawn mower around the yard.

In this dream I can afford a lawn mower.

Cold beer on the porch at night.

Lakeside kisses with the moon on the rise.

Mary

Once Mary told me she was pregnant, but first she asked where I saw us in five years.

I said, five years, how about ten?

I was working on a come-up, but it was gonna take some time.

There was an evening I stayed up late, waiting on Mary, so I crunched off chunks of Xanax and gnawed my nails to blood.

I said, Let's think fifteen years.

Rent overdue, bills to catch up on.

She said, What if I told you I was pregnant? And I was on my feet before I even realized.

We smoked but she dropped her smoke.

She laughed herself backward, tipped over the chair.

She said, Your face, your fucking face!

Earlier I had texted Mary as I waited, as I nibbled myself in anxiety, but she never did reply, only hustled in wearing Cracker Barrel blue, a bundle of stamp bags in her hand and we overdid it, maybe, because the good shit went too fast, lolling, neckless, boneless mass.

I said, If we scrimp and save, maybe twenty.

We didn't have any money.

I didn't ask her where she got the dope.

Sometimes she'd come home haggard, hit the shower and scrub forever, and I'd lie there naked, hard, and wait, and wait, and wait for her to never come out, until I drifted off.

She said, Not now. Not now.

She said, Why can't we just cuddle? Just hold my hand?

The Jeep Girl

I follow the yellow Wrangler to Circle K where she parks at the curb and the doors roll closed behind that angel of a Jeep Girl and I park my Buick at the fuel pump while next to me Mary stirs and mumbles herself awake and I draw out my debit card and think when it ticks up close to seven dollars I've got to cut off the pump and then I think eight more hours without a hit and it's gonna be gravel in my guts and sweats and shakes and restless legs so what's really the point and why am I even thinking about the Jeep Girl or some other soberer life and at the same time I wonder what's taking her so long like maybe she's waiting for me and planning our escape and I imagine a simple scene of pancakes in the breakfast nook and Mary says *where are we* and wonders do I need anything before she goes into the store and I wait and wait and decide whichever woman comes out first is my ride and for once in her life it's Mary armed with Funyuns and Gatorade and the pump reads seven thirty-five which means overdraft and the truck behind me honks.

And there's the Jeep always driving away.

Suboxone

Dime-sized hexagon stamped with a sword to defend
against the shivers and shits.

An orange pill, little blue bottle.

The doctor wouldn't fill the script unless her piss was opioid
free and sometimes Mary would be in there an hour waiting
down the line in the boarded-up strip mall next to Doctor
Luckey's *Cheap Vasectomies*, a head shop, and then empty
windows. And sometimes it would be even longer because the
doctor would say Mary was positive for dope.

Sometimes Mary had to beg.

It tasted like its color, medicine, chemicals, and powdered
tangerine, the opioid agonist chewed or sucked and then nothing nothing nothing.

She got in the car, tossed the bottle in her bag, and said,
Let's fucking go.

Ten, fifteen dollars per pill, sickly sweet, head leveled.

She said, Punch it, Chewie.

A thrum that melts like sugar on the tongue.

Punch it.

While we craved the vinegar of heroin.

The Jeep Girl

The road's nothing but a glint of sunshine and it's not even that when I lower my shades.

Mary

I'd like to tell you we loved each other.

Her hands were strong and on the way home she pinched my neck till I squirmed and soon the agony cut to relief as she pummeled my muscles to dough.

I said, I love you.

She said, Is everything okay?

Her fingers crawled along my shoulders, clawed at straps of wasted muscle and I thought about the Jeep Girl, our house, the simple totem of the mailbox, act of picking up the mail.

Mary said, *How's that feel?* and her fingers dug in, blanked my vision to red, and I was like *Okay. I'm good. Stop. Fuck. Stop.*

But she didn't stop.

When I looked, her body clenched and shook and I sped to the hospital while she foamed at the mouth and writhed against the belt that I unbuckled at the drop-off. I heaved her from the seat and I didn't know what to do. I couldn't get caught.

And I didn't love or hate her then.

I didn't anything her at all.

Heroin

Each time the needle pricked my skin, I felt that pinch of dread. I used to do this thing where I'd load up a shot and wait and wait until my body shook with want. And then I'd wait some more. And my nose would run and saliva would pool in my mouth.

The future's clock ticks like this: Dread. Hope. Dread. Hope. Dread. Dread. Dread.

Heroin

I'd like to tell you we can be normal and beautiful again, but now I'm nothing but a dapple of track marks, the Jeep's driven off, and Mary might as well be dead.

The day I chased the Wrangler was the day I dreamed of impossible cleanness, all those particles of future that, day by day, pinprick by pinprick, I can make disappear.

Me

The part of me that still thinks I killed Mary keeps driving by her parents' house, keeps calling them till the cops come. The cops say to leave it alone. They say, *Rehab, Death, or Prison.* And I'm like, *I know, I fucking know.* Because those are the options. And if Mary asked now, I'd say, Five years? Clean time, savings account, a two-story house. I'd say, Yes, I'll hold your hand.

I'd wait for the jolt.

Sever the Head

Everyone at Scusi Cellars is drunk before the rush, so I too gulp Cabernet to rosy up my cheeks, then I hoist my tray and serve the masses. I take my first table, a book club sans books who crowd two high-tops with juicy gossip. I lean into the tableful of ladies and let my tight slacks do their work. I say, French Kiss Viognier, Sweet Lips Gewürtz, a voluptuous, smooth, and buttery Chard. They stop their chatter, all attention on me. I catch them off guard with a vulgar joke. They order. I wink. I pop the cork. I'm working for tips, and tonight they're rolling in.

Back at the bar, Dunk waits with two shots of grappa like a fun, drunk uncle. He says, To Saturday night! and we touch glasses, slug the liquor. Then we prepare the flights. I say, Zin! and Dunk underhands me the bottle. He fumbles as I chuck it back, but recovers to a dribble of applause. We know that when our clientele of Midwest bourgeoisie ascend in the elevator from the cavern, when they blink into the late summer daylight that glints off Lake Erie and stumble to their convertibles or tour buses, off to the other wineries in Oldtown, they will remember us: clumsy Dunk and suave and sexy Sly. We're fun. We're seductive. We know our wine.

                         ~

I go to lay a smooch on Al when I get home that night, but he leans away and swivels back to pop weed chocolates from their molds onto the cooling rack. He gave up palming dime bags at dive bars when medical use passed last year and he has eyes on a permit, on storefront with a sign. No more secret stashes, no more sketchy glances at cops.

Al says, God, you smell like booze.

I say, Oh come on, boyo, I was celebrating.

I slap my wad of tips on the counter but Al doesn't even look. I've explained my condition to him before, how Doctor Dez suggests a couple shots a day to dampen my Intrusive Thoughts, but still Al gives me shit. He'd rather I toke myself into a red-eyed blob, but the booze warms me like weed never could. It smooths my inhibitions, dials up the charm. Plus it's my job to know which wines to recommend.

When Al isn't looking, I swipe a chocolate for my bath. He says, But you're still drying out after New Year's, right?

                         ~

Dunk says detox is pointless, says he used to sober up every year during Scusi's January shutdown. New Year's Day he'd fake a vacation, stock up on tomato juice, ice cream, and plenty of seltzer, lock the door and turn off all the lights. Anyways, he says, When you get back to work your tolerance is down and you wind up stumbling before dinnertime.

I've seen this personally. Once I dragged a drunken Dunk to the cellar's cot to sleep it off mid-shift, pulled a full house for two hours solo. But I'd like to think Dunk would do the same for me.

I'd like to think Dunk cares. I slip into the scalding water, drink out of a bottle of blended red, and relax. Al only wants me to sober up because his homophobic father used to chug Old Crow. But his dad was a dick before the booze, born again a pig. Al tells me I'm mean when I'm drunk, selfish, but he's just deflecting. As the water prunes me, I remember I have a job, an income. I support our way of life.

After my bath, I wrap myself in my ratty robe. Al's reading in bed and I kiss him on the cheek. He pecks me back. If I was selfish I'd lie down beside him, but I'm not. I care. I head to the couch because I can't help but keep him awake with my snores.

～

I discovered Doctor Dez about five years ago, after my bachelor's, while floundering in my parents' basement. Those days I didn't have a job and my alcohol dependence really was out of control. I started my day with no recollection of the night before, covered in bruises from fights or falls. I developed this strange habit of losing my clothes, of walking home barefoot and waking up nude. I would lie in bed through the afternoon worried I would ruin every relationship before it had a chance to flourish. So I cracked the vodka and pregamed. A fifth was all the confidence I needed to hit the bars and flirt.

I had these Intrusive Thoughts of physical violence, but Doctor Dez, with PhDs in Spirituality and Wisdom Studies, says that people like us aren't weak, but powerful, as long as we learn to control it. He calls us Supreme Empaths, more in tune with emotions, and this sensitivity is why Perpetrators of Evil are able to Intrude in our minds. On his YouTube channel, Doctor Dez says that Intrusiveness is often misdiagnosed:

Anxiety, Depression, Bipolar. He says medication leaves us hollow and void. But his exercises help us find our Holy Self and a strong sense of being able to fight back.

With Doctor Dez's guidance I began to manage my drinking, my weak sense of being. I got a job at Scusi's and learned to enjoy the flavors, the nose, to pick apart the colors and mouthfeels, respect the wine before each drink so I was *partaking*, not just getting drunk. That summer, Dunk invited me to the Festival at the Cliffs where we camped with some of his old Deadhead buddies which is where I met Al. He sold us magic mushrooms and we tripped throughout the night, wrapped in stoner light shows, and I felt the universe calm around the significant center of my Holy Self. With Doctor Dez's wisdom and Mr. Scusi's tutelage, I learned to control my Intrusive Thoughts. I moved in with Al to live a mostly normal life.

꙳

I can tell Dunk's already in his cups when we meet Mr. Scusi at the front door the next morning to press Cabernet. Dunk and I aren't morning people, and I'm hungover, squinting at the sun and Mr. Scusi's bright cherubic cheeks. He says, Cabernet! and gestures wildly at the world around us.

I say, Off to the dungeon! which brings head-splitting laughter to all, and we ride the elevator down to the cool vaulted cavern.

We get to work ladling fermented grape must into the press where the hydraulic rubber bladder smashes the skins against the sieve, the juice waterfalling into buckets. As Mr. Scusi watches the action, Dunk and I funnel containers of unaged wine into barrels. When a barrel is full, we bung it and roll it away to age in the musty back rooms. My stomach turns as we work, head ball-peened and ringing. An Intrusive Thought squeezes in and I see myself crush Dunk's body in the press, crunch of bone and blood oozing out of the spigot. I close my eyes and focus on my Holy Self, but the thoughts don't stop, and this time I shove Scusi himself into the barrel headfirst and roll it down the docks into the murk of Lake Erie.

After four barrels we break to clean the sieve. Mr. Scusi dips a glassful of the fresh unfiltered wine and passes it to me. First sip I feel the warmth shoot through me. I drink again and my skull loosens, eases into a fresh new day. I say, Is that black currant I taste?

Scusi swirls, sniffs, and swigs. Says, Tannic, dark fruit, wet gravel. He kisses his fingertips.

Dunk kills the wine. Refills. Re-kills. Mr. Scusi unsheathes a wine thief, unbungs a dust-smothered barrel, and suctions out a vintage draught. He holds the glass vial of grappa to the light, pleased with his premium barrel-aged reserve. He lifts his thumb and the liquid dribbles into his mouth. Dunk and I have waited on this barrel for years, eyeing the patinated iron straps, the indiscernible faded label. Scusi clicks his tongue at the taste, rolls his eyes, says, Not today. But almost. He hammers the bung back in.

Ten a.m. and we should be open but instead we're three wine enthusiasts edged up to the bar, slobbering with laughter over Mr. Scusi's latest run-in with the cops. Last week he was driving his Porsche the wrong way down Main Street when a semi turned left off Second into his path and he had to take to the sidewalk, cracking a telephone pole. This! He shows us a picture on his phone of the battered luxury car. Totaled!

Dunk says, Bet your wife was pissed.

But Scusi just says, Wife? Phhbt. I have money!

He lays a hundred-dollar bill for each of us on the bar before leaving.

∽

When I stretch up from the couch the next morning I'm greeted by the smell of pancakes and coffee, the living room a dazzle of sun, my blankets tossed on the floor. Al appears beside me and I say, Good morning, boyo. I try to open up a smile.

He says, Hope you had a good sleep. It's noon. Breakfast is cold, but I've got something to show you.

The thought of food makes me want to puke anyway. I say, Show.

Al sits and opens his laptop. He says, It would be a great getaway for both of us. They believe some of the same stuff as your Doctor Dez. Meditation. Finding yourself.

It's an email confirmation for a twenty-eight-day stay at an Ibogaine clinic in Juárez. I click on the website to read about third eyes, psychotropics, guru-guided souls searches. I scroll through the details. Thousands of dollars. I say, There's no way we can afford it.

He says, Well.

He says, Your parents agreed to chip in.

My parents? What the fuck do my parents have to do with it? They're coming over today so we can talk more.

And that's when I see it, right there on the home page: *This treatment alleviates symptoms of alcohol withdrawal and elevates the spiritual recovery from addictive substances.*

I say, Oh fuck no. You're sending me to rehab?

He tells me to listen, but I don't listen. I say, I told you I'd quit.

He says, Sly, babe, I'd like to trust you, but last night you pissed in the tub. I'm not going to get mad. I promised myself I wouldn't get mad.

I say, That's the problem. That's my condition. I drink so that I *don't* get mad.

He says, You always blame your *condition*. What's your *condition* and what is *you*?

I don't know what that means, but I close my eyes, stay level as my guru. I keep breathing while I look for my keys. He whines some more as I get in the car, as I keep the windows closed and back my Buick out of the drive.

In fifteen minutes I'm deep in the bustle of Oldtown, twenty and I'm taking the elevator down. Scusi Cellars has employee showers and a back room stocked with clothes and towels. There's wine on the bar with my name on it. There's everything I need.

∽

Mondays are slow, so Dunk and I shoot grappa and I bitch about my lover and Dunk philosophizes, wise and careless, about love being a passing thing. It's going on 11 p.m. and the closed sign's been out an hour and I continue to ignore Al's texts about how we need to talk and where am I?

And am I ok?

And am I coming home tonight?

I leave my phone under the counter and walk off to smarm the couple who have been here three hours but don't want their thirtieth wedding anniversary to end. They say, This booth! Right here! This was before your time, but he got down on one knee and it was just a plastic mood ring because that's all we could afford. They say, Sorry to keep you over, but it's our anniversary!

They are drunk.

I think, *this is love*.

I tell them it's no trouble. And it's not except I struggle with Intrusive Thoughts where I bash their skulls in with a chair. Each time my phone goes off my anxiety shifts into a higher gear, and I imagine eviscerating Dunk before I set him on fire. I look at the last of eleven messages: *I'm worried, babe. Just let me know your fine.* I can't take it. I refill my glass.

While I scrub the last of the dishes, Dunk holds up a carafe to check for spots and his eyes tremble closed before he timbers stiffly over. He smacks his skull on the sink and stemware shatters on his body, on the ground. I reach out as he falls, too far away for me to do anything. I stand over him saying, Fuck! Dunk! You okay? But he doesn't even mumble, just shakes and finally stills. He makes the smallest, cutest fart that echoes its way to silence.

My phone vibrates with another fucking text from Al: *Please tell me your not dead. Should I call 911?* I swipe his dramatic bullshit away and call the ambulance myself.

Doctor Dez says to know your limits. I don't know where to find a pulse. I don't know CPR. I have no clue how to save a life. The couple leaves cash on the table and jets with apologies while I watch Dunk's breath run shallow. Then it finally stops. All alone with his empty body and all I can do is wait. I turn off my phone and drink from the bottle, remembering Dunk's dirty jokes, his avuncular advice. I think of the time a patron grabbed his ass and the look on his face and I laugh. Then I chug. Heady oak notes, up-front tannins.

When the bottle's about halfway gone, Dunk gasps and opens his eyes. I lift his head and trickle some booze into his mouth. I say, Don't worry. The ambulance is on the way. He spits up purple on his shirt.

Minutes later he's on a stretcher disappearing through the elevator doors. One paramedic stays behind to get his info, but there's no wallet, only a wad of cash. I can't even remember his full name, just Dunk. I gulp dregs from the bottle. This paramedic is blond and youthful. He asks if I can drive. I slump and slur. I say, How bout you give me a ride, boyo? But his look doesn't change. He says, Maybe you better call your boss.

Sometime after I've wiped down the anniversary couple's table and closed up for the night, I'm sitting in the parking lot beneath the fluorescent light watching docked pontoons bob and buoy when Al appears to help me up and I retch my guts into the brickwork. He catches my fist as I swing it at his chest, listens to me curse every name that comes to mind. I curse the way the water always smells like fish and I curse the group that stops to nudge one another before barhopping their way along the drag. Al drives me home, crutches me to bed, takes off my clothes, and I fade into sleep while he holds me close.

I tell Al that of course Dunk's heart attack was a wake-up call, and I try to cut back over the next couple weeks. The grapes have all been processed into barrels, drawing oak from the Bulgarian wood, and I sample sparingly through my shift. The night before Scusi's end of season party, I'm a bit tipsy after work, nothing crazy, when I tell Al, Sure, boyo, I can make it through the party sober. I'll just eat a chocolate if things get rough. I tell him it will be a test. If I can do this on my own, we'll tell my parents Juárez is off.

Al says, I trust you, babe.

The winery closes down for this one day every November and I spend my day off sleeping in. Around noon I pour a cup of kombucha from the fridge, watch as Al mixes his chocolate in the kitchen wearing only briefs and a frilly thrifted apron. If I could freeze this moment I would, keep this kind of peace, a comfortable house, a steady job, stable love. But then in the shower I can't stop thinking about hard seltzer and I wonder if maybe I am too far gone. Maybe I've overindulged. But then I remember how Doctor Dez says not to give in to uncertainty.

He also pushes the Supreme Power of the Mind. I breathe. I focus. My Holy Self can accomplish anything.

When I walk out of the bathroom, I drop the towel. Al's at the foot of the bed wearing nothing under the apron now. He says, Kiss the cook? And the apron falls, and we become just limbs and bodies, all thought evicted, all kisses and touch. We breathe together. We make each other windless.

We shower again once we've untangled, leave the apron on the bedroom floor, wash the wonderful sweat and stink of each other off one another's body. I think of the grappa, the burn of it, warm as a blanket, a reward, but there's nothing in the house. All the alcohol is gone.

～

Since I'm not drinking, we take my car to the party, stop-and-go traffic through the bustle of an Oldtown that's cooling into winter. We get stuck behind the pedal-powered mobile bar filled with frozen frat boys tying one on. We inch by Jimmy Buffet burger bars, overfull tiki drinks, dance parties of blinking lights.

When Al and I take the elevator down to Scusi, the cavern is black tie, a hardwood table in the center of the room rimmed with high-backed chairs. I imagine we are entering a castle, the echoic ancient ceiling and party guests grouped by caste. Dunk and I hang with the waitstaff at the bar while the kitchen all bundles together in their own corner and Mr. Scusi's coterie of wealthy sycophants circle his wife in the center of the room, complimenting each other's suits and dresses. Mr. Scusi himself perambulates with the caterers who hoist platters of fist-sized shrimp, caviar, champagne, and cocktails.

Dunk tells the story of what it's like to be dead for two minutes. He says, Sly's the man! This dude saved my life. He raises a glass to me, and Al squeezes my hand as I hoist my water in response. Once Dunk moves onto his next story, I excuse myself to the restroom. I straighten my tie, splash water on my face. I'm sweating, but not hot. I wipe myself with a fistful of paper towels.

I open the door to Mr. Scusi mid-knock who proffers a snifter of viscous pink liquid. He says, It is ready! He says, Drink. Drink. He hands me the glass and says, Finish it.

This is what Mr. Scusi's been keeping from us, a small batch of ancient high gravity liquor finished in port barrels to smooth its edge. I can't imagine saying no. Just a sip. The liquid moves through me, toes to fingertips, blessed elixir. I breathe in air after a day underwater and I take another drink, swishing before I swallow. I sip one final time, then hide the drink behind my back, waiting, watching Al at the bar.

When Mr. Scusi returns, though, he won't take back the booze. He snatches a flute from a tray and flicks his fingernail against it, rings the room to silence. His wife comes to stand beside him and he opens his arms to everyone as the kitchen doors swing wide. Scusi says, Pièce de résistance! and out comes the chef followed by two waiters balancing a tray with an octopus the size of a small child wriggling wildly. Red tentacles grip and pull, suction and slither, dragging the blob of head toward the edge.

The cellar inhales, all except for Al who glares over the masses as I hold my drink up to toast this masterpiece. I try to look away, to hide. I'm too late. I blush, but Scusi's hand is on my shoulder, and I can't move as the chef, bearded and toqued, describes the preparation, a Cabernet braise, fresh sea salt. He strops a scimitar-sized knife. He says, The beauty is in its simplicity. We prepare the octopus fresh, as soon as we sever the head!

There is applause and then there's chatter. When I turn back toward Al, he is gone.

Pools of people gather like mercury bubbles around shrimp and olives. At the bar Dunk is loaded, and he tilts into the service area where the one interested waitress still listens. Neither know where Al went. But he can't be gone because I still have the keys. I weave toward the elevator, but Mr. Scusi blocks my path.

He says, My boy! This way! He hugs me toward the kitchen. And there it is, the octopus, splayed on a sterilized table like an alien body, limbs held down by sous chefs, restrained for biopsy. Bodies pack in behind me. The chef is beside me, slaps me on the back. His black hair curls around his toque and his eyes spark with something wild. He holds the scimitar, slaps the blade against his palm, then clasps it between two praying hands, handle at my chest. Scusi says, Sly, you must do the honors!

The room watches, waits for me to breathe, but my breath is caught, then it's heavy and fast. I don't know what to do. The chef says, Yes you do. The head. He makes a motion somewhere between a slice and a saw. And in that moment the thoughts intrude, a battlefield of bloodied kitchen staff, the octopus now with Al's soft mouth, and the blade trembles in my hands. Scusi says, To Sly! The man of the hour!

I am pit-stained, shaking, undone, and the octopus is Al and I am his slayer and I cock back. I am in control of none of this. I am hacking through him, cutting the tentacled spectacle to chum. There is applause and then there is silence.

∽

We barely talk on the flight, but Al holds my hand as I gulp down airplane bottles of Sutter Home over ice to stop the shakes. Once we've made it through customs we take a cab to the clinic where we sign our names a dozen times. The orderlies let us strip together, fill separate lockers with our belongings and take our valuables to the safe. They check our bodies for contraband, and I watch Al lift his junk, spread his cheeks, then I follow suit. We are naked for our goodbye kiss and then we're given bathrobes and led to separate, windowless rooms.

I lie in a bed as soft as rain and I wait for the door to open, for the guru to appear. I imagine a man like Doctor Dez offering the dose, or me tipping back the Ibogaine ramekin to Scusi's wild gestures. Or maybe this guru's more wise and bumbly, like the burned-out blaze of Dunk. But then I realize he'll be just another man I've never met who doesn't know me. He'll ask how I'm feeling and he'll offer up the cup. He'll say, Are you ready? Do you wish to change your life? My body will be helpless, worry flecked around a center of hope, and I will answer. All set.

Digging

On my first date with Tucker we sat in my car and watched a house burn. The firefighters tried to coax a pit bull from the second-floor window but the dog only circled and howled at the flames. It dodged and snapped at their Kevlar gloves. Ash snowed over my CRV's windshield and I felt the okayness of Tucker's hand on my knee, his pulse when he squeezed. I'd drifted from campus to campus, then from state to state since after grad school, chasing underpaid adjunct jobs. I was always uncertain and always alone, but Tucker's touch was an anchor. He held me there. Westinghouse, Ohio. I didn't want to leave.

I couldn't look away from the roar of the flames, the shouts of the crew on the ground who jetted water through the front door, the man on the ladder who stretched precariously through the window grasping for the collar. The dog snarled. It whipped its head and its mouth foamed, locked up by deep-rooted fear.

My commute took me past this house often. This side of town featured absentee landlords, fallen porticoes. I'd roll through slowly, scope the relics, before hanging a right toward downtown where they'd turned a century-old mill into the lofts I called home. Before the house fire, the dog trudged muddy circles in the yard and I used to think, *this dog is me*. We understood each other in our limited listlessness.

But that night, the night of the fire, the dog escaped. It locked its jaws around the firefighter's arm, tumbling with him, bouncing down the ladder rungs. When the ball of man and dog struck ground, they untangled, stumbled, dizzy, mad, confused. Then the pit took off, evaporated itself into the night.

↶

Before the fire, I'd met Tucker at the Tequila Saloon where I celebrated each weekend with too many shots. When I was drunk enough, I'd hit on straight dudes till the bartender cut me off. I bought Tucker a drink and flirted as was my wont, and the bartender slid a finger across his throat, a warning. But he couldn't see it was too late, that under the counter, Tucker kneaded my inner thigh.

Back at my place, we stripped out of our smoky clothes. Tucker gripped my hair and I thought about how I used to confuse the words *ravage* and *ravish*, how I whispered *ravage me* into a lover's ear and how sometimes *ravage* felt closer to what I craved. This was our first night together. I was wonderfully destroyed.

After we fucked, I expected Tucker to make up some excuse and leave. I'd resigned myself to that loss. I curled into the cool wall's comfort and waited, but instead he angled into me, asked what I'd like for breakfast. I snuggled deeper into his big spoon, found comfort there, his rough skin, ferocious warmth.

I was amazed when he was still with me a month later. His mid-twenties restless energy shook me from my early-thirties slump. He'd thrown off careers and college to busk and train-hop.

He called abandoned buildings home. While I whined about the transience of academic contract jobs, the interstate moves required by my academic career, Tucker preached the doctrine of the unbound, the freedom of not being tied down. He was proud of his depravity, his wild head of unwashed hair, while I wore my normative career, my pleated slacks, and gut in a shame I couldn't shake.

৹

A few weeks later at the Tequila Saloon, Tucker scraped his stool next to mine and, though he pulled our palms beneath the bar, I still felt the warmth between us, even if he was too afraid to reveal it to the world.

He asked how my day was and I complained about Non-traditional Nadia, a student who, though she was my age, prefaced most comments in class with *You're probably too young to remember this*. Ever since I was a child, I dealt with anxiety that manifested itself in an endless fountain of sweat. I wore cardigans to hide my pit stains, carried extra undershirts in my car. And it was like my students could see through me, their beautiful bodies mocking my dad bod, my purely utilitarian fashion, the dampness, the uncertainty. I said, Sometimes I wonder why I ever pursued my English degree. I'm not a professor.

I stopped, worried my whining would scare Tucker off. Dim lights. Slow music. Tucker shook his head. It's them, not you, babe. You're perfect.

He had something to tell me, but not there. At home, he said, meaning my home, our home, a private place that we, together, shared. He had to stop by his dealer's on the way and asked to borrow a fifty toward his eight ball, but I didn't care. I could be the provider, the caretaker, as long as he held me close.

Tucker's touch, his small kindnesses, they grounded me.

As he snorted a blizzard of cocaine from my coffee table, Tucker began to ramble. He told me about how back in the fifties the Westinghouse PD performed a gay sex sting on these underground bathrooms below the Westinghouse square. The police hid a camera and several officers behind a two-way mirror and when the businessmen or bankers or brewers dropped their drawers, when they fell to their knees in front of one another to worship each other's bodies, the cops would bust out, would beat them, sometimes to death.

It's all on video, he said. And some of those cops are still out there, alive and free.

Due to backlash against police brutality and the legality of the sting, the bathroom was backfilled two months later, and it was rumored that several bodies remained buried in their lavatorial graves. The city had moved on, stashed away the tapes, hid its past, and now hosted pride parades as if they'd always been accepting, always done their best.

I said, We should make those motherfuckers pay. But there wasn't much emotion behind the words. I was glad that typical midcentury homophobia was behind us. It was sad to lose those men to violence, I said. But they died so we could express who we are.

Tucker started to speak and then stopped. He tried again, a whisper. I've done some bad shit in my life, he said.

It's fine, I said. It's over.

I was such a bully. His tears shimmered. I was such a dick.

I said, The past is the past. You're fine. We're fine.

We could make them pay, he said. Would you like that? We could unearth the evidence. I could prove it.

Prove what?

He passed me the rolled twenty-dollar bill and I took a bump, only enough to make the blood rush around my body.

Tucker turned toward me, worked the buttons of my Oxford, gave up and yanked it over my head.

I could prove I've changed. I'm not ashamed, he said.

I peeled off my undershirt and used it to wipe the dampness from my armpits. He grabbed me by the hips. The coke had us babbling, spewing secrets. His mouth on my collarbone, I told him he was doing enough, that this moment was sufficient, the most love I'd felt in a decade.

Suspicion crept in and I began to wonder if I was only an experiment, because at this point it felt like more, but that was a question for another time. It didn't matter when his hand went from gentle to tight around my throat as his mouth worked its way down my torso, as he began to unbutton my jeans.

～

I googled the underground bathroom during office hours. Not much official, but the rumors ranged from ten to twenty prominent men gone missing during the length of the sting. There was one journalist working on an exposé, criticizing the legality of the operation. A false wall built into the bathroom without being cleared by the law director. Unsigned warrants, inadmissible evidence, but before he could piece it all together, the journalist hanged himself. The message boards cited strange circumstances surrounding the suicide.

Through chat rooms Tucker found a digital copy of a few clips from the evidence reel, black-and-white blowjob footage shot by cop voyeurs. Tucker plugged in the flash drive. He swiped his hair behind his ears, put his head on my lap and pressed play.

The cops revealed their two-way mirror, their secret room. They grinned like fifth-grade bullies mid-pummeling. There was a tour of the bathroom, a shot of the staircase that led to the depths, the false wall. I flinched when Tucker snatched my hand and squeezed it. I looked into his face, the curls of unruly beard, the way his eyes moonbeamed, his lips plump in a nest of mustache. He was homeless, but he was also out of my league. At that moment I thought he loved me.

I love you, I said.

On the screen two haloed figures met at the mouth and one dropped to his knees. The man who stood looked at the musty ceiling like it was filled with bright rapture. The other man smiled and went down.

I wanted to believe Tucker said he loved me too, but his face was in my lap, his response muffled by my thigh.

That night when I slept, I drifted into the bathroom beneath the city square. My hand caressed Tucker's scalp, pulled his face into my groin. I raised my head, but there was no heavenly bliss for me. Faceless students judged me from the ceiling joists and Tucker disappeared. The man behind the mirror laughed. It was Tucker's laugh. I woke to silence, an empty bed. He had gone sometime in the night.

❧

I called Tucker after class but his phone was off and when I checked the usual spots where he played acoustic power ballads for spare change, they were vacant. Two months and we'd spent most nights together, shared breakfasts, discussed our hopes and dreams. Whatever we had, I was to blame for losing it. Maybe that *I love you* was too strong, too much to commit to. A week went by and I tried to fill the void, hit the Tequila Saloon every night, but he was never there.

I took a walk one Sunday while the rest of the town sang hymns. I passed along the railroad tracks on the North End and looked for Tucker's tags. He'd explained his transience to me as a lack followed by a promise of home, but he said Westinghouse had been his longest stay. As a rambler he'd broken many hearts. He'd wooed and then abandoned a great many lovers but in Westinghouse, with me, he sought a philosophical change. I looked for the scrawl of his initials that would last for years, that I couldn't erase. I huffed as I walked. I sweated through my hoodie. My phone vibrated and I gasped in a breath as I answered Tucker's call. I asked if he was okay. But he told me to chill. He had something to show me. He wanted to meet me. Midnight. Behind the Saloon.

I covered my balding head with a knit cap and followed Tucker from the bar through an alley. He was more fucked up than usual and he chain-smoked as he hustled me along. I pinched his butt and he slapped my hand. He said, Come on. This way.

The brickwork undulated, this hollowed out town. In the wake of its heyday of factories, breweries, even a famous cult, it was reduced to a few dive bars and shadow. Tucker stopped and I saw that we stood in the back of the old Worlinger Building, three floors that towered over the pitted street. I followed him to the basement, cement pillars, my phone's flashlight not strong enough to reach the distant walls. There was a wheelbarrow filled with digging implements in the room's center, a pile of dirt that summited five feet from the floor. Tucker stood by the wall where sandstone bricks the size of people had been removed, replaced by a plywood door which he pulled aside to reveal a tunnel burrowed into blackness. He said, This is it.

I said, This is what?

I've been digging for a month. I didn't want to tell you until

I was sure, and, well. He used his flannel to wipe the grease from his brow. I made it. I'm there.

It took me a minute. I said, The bathroom?

Tucker beamed. He was lunatic with delight.

I said, Holy shit.

I said, Why? I peered down the tunnel. It was a straight shot to darkness and beyond that darkness, a greater depth.

I told you that I'd make things right, he said, I had to make things right.

I heard a tab pop, then another and when I turned, I was faced with a tallboy of shit beer.

I've never been with a dude before you, man. I should have told you, but I didn't want to ruin it.

Okay? I said. It was no big deal. Everyone starts somewhere. I forced a smile.

I used to be such a dick, he said. I bullied the shit out of this one kid, and, well. … And I've been feeling so guilty since I've been with you and, well, shit. I thought, how can I *prove* it?

You don't need to prove anything, I said. You just need to be there.

He didn't hear me. Or he ignored me. Tucker was wild-eyed, dancing, bouncing up and down. I'm gay, man! I'm out. I'm queer, I'm here. Get used to it.

I didn't sip my beer. I thought of the nights I'd called, the energy I'd depleted wandering the town, looking for answers, convincing myself that, even if Tucker was gone, I was still worthy of love.

You didn't have to prove anything, I said again. And this time he heard me. He stopped. You didn't have to do anything but be there, motherfucker. You just had to be there.

Tucker faced me, lazy eyes angled at my peripheries. Hair matted, face flecked with dirt. Are you fucking kidding me? he said. Are you fucking for real? All this work!

I didn't ask you, I said. I didn't want.

I ducked to avoid his beer can, then a second can zinged by on the other side.

I worked my ass off for you. He said, What do you want? A million dollars? A mansion with a swimming pool? A Lamborghini?

He continued his list, his voice fading as I ran, cut off when I burst through the door, slammed it behind me, collapsed into the Worlinger parking lot choking on tears.

⌒

On my commute I passed the house now burnt to only a heap of ash. The city parked a backhoe over the wreckage, but the backhoe never moved, and the rain came and went, and the ground settled.

I blocked Tucker's number. The semester ended and I focused on the four classes' worth of final papers awaiting grades. I didn't drink or smoke or snort, but I still let myself go. I ate family-sized bags of potato chips, scavenged my cupboards for snacks, and when there were no snacks left, I made midnight trips to Circle K. I filled myself with Polar Pops and the promise of my students' futures, a diversity of possible politicians, writers, and pop stars burgeoning out of my classroom. In my stupid way, I hoped they liked me. But it didn't matter. I was fine on my own.

Once I'd posted grades, I celebrated at the Tequila Saloon and the bartender comped my first round. I watched Tucker in the back bar mirror as he passed by. He didn't notice me. He ordered two PBRs and two shots of Jack, though I only ever knew him to chug IPAs on my tab. I watched him bounce out to the patio. A runnel of sweat tickled down my side. I thought of the time when I apologized to Tucker for the reek of my shoes and he pulled off his own Timbs and said, You want to compare? A gesture. A joke. For two months he'd convinced me I wasn't revolting and now he was gone. He was selfish. He'd only wanted me to love him so he could forgive himself.

I ordered my own Jack and PBR and redownloaded Grindr but kept fucking up the password. I ordered another round, listened to Tucker's laugh trickle through the patio door. The oncoming summer heat and humidity carried his noise. There was another round and another, too many for me to drive. When I stumbled out the door, I wandered sans destination, watched the entire town of Westinghouse wobble and lurch. And after some time the booze wore away and I found myself standing in the Worlinger's loom. I was soaked, sticky with sweat. When I got to the roof I balanced on the rim and watched the sparse traffic pulse through the light below.

Tucker said my name from behind me. Neil. Neil. A word subsumed and spat back out.

Tucker said, Neil! What the fuck are you doing here?

I told him I quit my job and was homeless now too. I thought I'd move in, I said. There's plenty of room. I hopped off the edge, stepped toward him. His face was red and his left eyelid twitched with rage. He said, We aren't doing this, man. Not tonight.

His hair was matted. The wind couldn't move it. His jeans were paint-spattered, black T-shirt browned from wear. My own hair flowed wild as wheat fields, my chest necklaced by fresh sweat, but I was cleanish. I said, What did you *want*?

He let the question hang and the wind whipped it around. He said, I don't know, man. I—

A woman tripped through the doorway, recovered and said, Tuck-y! Is this your friend? I'm Jade. Come on, she said, holding up a baggie. There's plenty for all.

⌒

In the vault we sat around a teetering card table where Jade broke up lines on a jewel case, *Bob Seger's Greatest Hits*, and Tucker and I glared. Jade scraped the cocaine, passed the album to Tucker and said, Who's gonna snort Seger's dick? She had crafted a cocaine cock that bent between Seger's power stance.

In that case, Tucker said. Here, Neil.

You're such a giver, I said. Both with dicks of cocaine and—

Quit it, he said sharply. But he looked at Jade with fear in his eyes.

Jade said, I'm sensing some history.

Tucker said, Nothing serious. Bender buddies.

I said, Oh? I didn't realize.

He said, What?

I said, What are you trying to prove?

Nothing, he said. What are you trying to prove?

What would I need to prove? I have a life, I said. And a shower.

He said, Fuck you.

You wish, I said, and I snagged the Greatest Hits from Tucker, leaned into Bob Seger's dick and snorted up the line, kept going toward the pile over the rock legend's shoulder, continued to inhale till I choked on a clump, and I coughed, sprayed spittle and cocaine. I buried myself in the blow.

Whoa, whoa, whoa! Jade stood. We all did. Tucker pinched my shoulder to the bone. Jade said, The actual fuck?

Tucker, as brittle as ice, said: You motherfucker.

Dude, said Jade. Chill. I'm not even mad, but that was like a whole gram. You gotta make yourself puke. Blow your nose. Blow it.

I blew it. A white clot and then the vomit followed. The world tipped and I sprayed Tucker's shoe. My heart helicoptered, blades spun up my spine to my mind, caught on words and chopped them into senseless characters. I spoke and only mumbled. Blackness, then blinding light. I vomited again. Ecstasy and pain. Time passed or it didn't.

At some point Tucker smoothed my hair. I was lying down, and he kissed my furnace of a forehead. He breathed the words *I love you*, or maybe he didn't. My veins pumped. Either the couch or the sleeping bag smelled like humus, cigarettes, and patchouli, a garbage that I wanted to be wrapped in, that felt deserved. Thoughts of a far-off morning waft of breakfast, an arm around my flabby body. Jade laughed on the far side of the room and Tucker joined in. Their bodies rustled in his sheets. There were moans. I would wake with a headache, with no clue where I was. I'd emerge. Go home alone. Again. I was okay.

∽

It was June, summer classes in full swing, but I was packing my office's shelves into boxes when I turned to see Nontraditional Nadia in the room. She shut the door behind her and sat down. She said, I hear you met my friend Jade.

I blinked a gibberish of Morse code.

Nadia said, I mean, dude, we all have a life outside here. And I'm not your student anymore.

I said, Wow.

I said, Fuck.

Nadia said, Just thought you should know if you want any more of that shit.

I tried to say no, to say coke's really not my thing, especially now, but she fished a pen out of her purse, dropped my paper rubric onto the desk and wrote her number in the blank corner. She got up to leave but turned back. And, oh. Here's another sample to remind you. She tossed the baggie on the desk, and I scrambled to hide it before she opened the door and left.

Back at home, I changed into shorts and laced my Asics, kicked off into the late afternoon. I went shirtless for the tan, letting my diminishing fat wobble. My sweat flowed freely. I ignored everyone, shut the world out. I thought only of how the wind felt against my skin. I thought of the coke and Nadia's number becoming buried in junk mail. The summer stretched in front of me, the road, the rest of my life. I hadn't renewed my lease, never signed my contract to teach in the fall.

I imagined Tucker, wild-eyed, digging, his plan to exhume the past, to bring it into the present. And all I ever wanted was to be held, to edge back up next to him, the comfort of body on body and skin on skin and none of our self-loathing between us.

Was that too much to ask?

I ran past the demolished house, now a vacant lot, all the ashes and rubble hauled away and a fresh stubble of new grass poking through the straw. I stopped, backtracked. A swath of stalks had been kicked away and there were paw prints in the mud.

I smiled.

I ran.

I slipped into a daydream where I kept on running, out of town, over the train tracks, to the interstate and beyond. I broke through some barrier and left it all behind.

Spit Backs

Recovery

We found each other on Hope House Grads, the group Jean adminned for those of us who conquered the program's residential care, who tangoed through withdrawals on pressboard bunks and chain-smoked sleepless nights away, all of us who eventually graduated, separated, lost to our own individual lives, so we clicked accept on cautious friend requests and check-marked tentative follows and we reconnected with recovery buddies because now that addiction was behind us and our bodies and minds were healed, we craved community again, and we posted about our passions, movements, and ideologies and at first we shrugged off the rifts that erupted via political rant or sarcastic meme, but over time we learned to unfollow those friends we once hugged the tightest, shocked at so-and-so's gun-toting tirade or what's-his-name's socialist posts, and we were baffled that we survived those ninety days together, pumped iron as fascist spotted leftist, as the anarchist coached the future cop, and we wondered how these new political identities overwhelmed us while each unfollow hung heavy as an overdose, the covered-over hole of a lost-to-drugs friend.

Recovery

Jean is three years clean as he curves down the exit ramp, Volkswagen brimming with window-high stacks of books and planners, floor scattered with note cards, pens, files, his video camera, his entire life and nearly ninety-nine hours of footage from interviews with the fifty-two survivors of the opioid epidemic who'd responded to his Hope House Grads Facebook group and replied to his post, ninety-nine hours of audiovisual folklore Jean has collected over this past year of coast-to-coast travel, while he lived off grants and ramen, slept in roach motels in many and various cities and states, where the ex-addicts offered their firsthand accounts for a documentary which Jean hopes to complete over the next year while shacked up at his mother's, scraping by now that the grant money's gone, the advance dwindled, and he feels like his lifeline is a few inches of progress that's now rubber-banded back, a dream of serious groundbreaking work he wakes from, alert and disoriented in his childhood twin bed.

Recovery

However much our philosophies rankled each other, we banned politics on Hope House Grads, shared milestones and memories, self-help and sideline cheers, and our comments were all encouragement, congratulations that showered screens in stars, but mostly we clamored around Jean's project, liked and loved each update post, watched interview clips and transcribed quips from our cohorts proliferate on the web, and these were Jean's stories, our stories, some from anonymous shadows and others blatantly named, and we empathized and understood, teared up and smiled, omg-ed and lol-ed.

Recovery

Jean's first run-in with the man named _____ is at the meeting where Jean collects his two-year coin which is toward the tail end of Jean's final year of grad school in Westinghouse, Ohio, the basement of the Episcopalian church where the woman who leads the meetings bangs the Big Book, squeezes a rubber chicken, and lets a buckaw douse the ten of them in ruberified air while Jean is just antsy for a smoke break where, as he chain-smokes, _____ claws onto Jean's arm and asks him if he has a sponsor, which Jean doesn't, but he hesitates because of _____'s urgency, something familiar in the way _____'s sly eye lingers, so Jean lies, I'm sorry, I've already got one, and _____ looks disappointed, stares at Jean across the table through the second half of the meeting where Jean ratchets his noisemaker half-assedly and someone else blows a whistle and others emit various sounds to celebrate the weirdness of recovery, the diversity of once floundering bodies freshly rehabbed, progressing.

Recovery

Jean's car growls by cornfields and the Hell Is Real billboard, past hawk after hawk taloned to fence posts, Midwest as fuck, just like the Rust Belt, the opioid epidemic itself, and he listens to NPR gab on about the hurricane building strength in the Atlantic, ripe for landfall in the gulf, possibly bigger than Katrina, its predicted course locked on Clearwater which makes Jean think back three years to Hope House, to meeting his buddy Louis who's now on Facebook but has never responded to Jean's online invite, who, for all Jean knows, still works at the rehabilitation center with no other place to go, nothing but infrequent nu metal on Louis's timeline, and now that music's ugly crunch clashes with Jean's predilection for a neoclassical wash, and now Jean is different and he wants to reach out, to connect more deeply than this gossamer of social media algorithms, to relive their shared history of sneaking into the chow hall to steal ice cream bars from the rehab's fridge.

Withdrawal

The first thing Jean did after he left Hope House and returned to the Midwest, after he tracked down a meeting, was to make a drive-by of the methadone clinic where he spent a good chunk of his early adulthood waiting in line to tip back the ramekin of liquid opioid agonist in front of the nurse only to turn and spit the stuff back out, stomach boiling through withdrawal, and he'd seal the legal dope in the cup to sell for negligible cash to some junkie because spit backs were easy money when he was under twenty-six and still on his parents' insurance and anyway, rumor had it that methadone ate an addict's bones (e.g. one interviewee had arthritis before thirty and ten others mentioned joint and bone issues after methadone use), but now, rehabilitated, as Jean drove by the boarded-up clinic, his own wrists ached and he slowed, steered closer to read the hopeful graffiti, *Moving Forward*, one of the faded town's most prolific tags, which was proof to Jean that the hurt he left behind was also, always, in front of him.

Relapse

Years later we gathered to watch outtakes of Jean's interview with his best friend Louis where Louis described his heroin high as *fixing something broken without the pain of having to heal*, and he referred to the Hope House Institute's holistic approach as a *sly way to rope-a-dope a motherfucker into lukewarm religion* which, this religion was something he raged against until he eventually succumbed to some half-assed attempt at piety, because we all were told we needed an ersatz god to confess to, something to which we could turn over our wills, but then Louis went on to talk about the night he shaped pillows into the form of his body beneath the sheets and made it as far as the Walgreens, had the needle in his arm when they tracked him down and dragged him back, locked and monitored him in the more secure withdrawal unit so he wouldn't influence his best friend Jean, and soon after Jean held up his completion plaque and took the bus back north and Louis had to sign a contract for work-study (which in the interview he called *indentured servitude*) while we all graduated and moved on to AA meetings and moral inventories and questions about our faith, while we diverged and disappeared, leaving Louis to struggle on his own.

Recovery

Unpacking his car into Mom's basement feels, to Jean, like an incipient stage of downward spiral and over the next few days he corkscrews lower, sleeps in and transcribes, isolates themes from drug narratives, but he mostly just watches the interviews blur into daydreams, hurricanes twiddling around in the gulf before crashing into the Hope House compound, bodies flung and rubble tumbled, and he feels the sudden urge to open Facebook, check Louis's profile where he finds a completely irrational pro-gun meme, but he opens the messenger app anyways and types *Howdy dude*, before he questions whether he, Jean, is the type of person to use the word *howdy* (only one interviewee addresses the camera with *howdy*, while the rest use *hey*, *hi*, and one *good morning*) so he finally x-es out of messenger and slumps back, less fit these days to deal with the present temporality the world now expects of him.

Relapse

Under every skirt's a slip, says _____, as his talons once
again dig into Jean's shoulder, a protector, _____ reminds
him, an open ear, and this reprimand is all because Jean tried to
flirt with the newcomer, a woman with the tattoo of a magnolia
flower blooming on her throat, and even though Jean used to
be too anxious to *put himself out there*, now that he isn't drunk
or high, now that he's finished a graduate degree in folklore and
spends five days a week at the gym, his mind seems to work
faster, his body firmer, skin smoother, teeth brushed to a flash,
and for once he's begun to notice women stealing glances, and he
recently caught that glint of attraction in Magnolia's shadowed
eyes, so he chats her up on smoke breaks which _____ calls
Thirteen Stepping, the first step of being powerless combined
with the twelfth, sharing this powerlessness with others, and
all of this after years where sex was a craving buried deep by
opioid need, and now that the drive is awake inside him, Jean
finds himself cockblocked by Twelve Step clichés.

Recovery

We were giddy as we followed the hurricane on live feeds where the storm made landfall and crumpled Hope House stucco, washed it back out to sea, and a couple weeks later we shared articles that spurned the Hope House founder who'd embezzled money, siphoned donations, etcetera, the founder who had recently gone missing though none of this surprised us because we'd all seen the shady paperwork, all signed ambiguous contracts, and we couldn't entirely hate the man either because his program, his Hope House, was the reason why many of us were alive, but we also didn't mourn his loss because now we had Jean and Hope House Grads, because we had community and anyways, wasn't it like karma that after all our drug-addled scams we would be the ones scammed?

Relapse

Jean nods at his computer, four in the morning and the messenger screen still open with a stupid *howdy dude* sent in its blue bubble when Louis messages, *Yo what was that song you liked back when u was at Hoe House that sad shit about shooting dope* (*Hoe House* appearing as a nickname for the rehab in thirty-three interviews) and Jean is transported from his current body into the scrawny weird one he lived in only thirty days after withdrawal, but the song is still elusive, could be anything from Velvet Underground to Elliott Smith, a bundle of real downers that once enlightened him by sharing traumatic moments of needles and urges, so Jean splurges, shares link after YouTube link of these songs that bring him back to the old Jean, the Jean with bangs, dressed all in black instead of khakis and button-downs, but none of these are the song Louis wants so Jean writes, *how is life and everything, I'm still in boring ass Ohio, you still at Hoe House* and Louis says, *packing and getting a playlist ready trying to take off tomorrow to beat the hurricane U kno the one about a hole in my arm where the money goes*, which makes Jean wonder why Louis didn't google those lyrics, why Louis even wrote him back at all.

Recovery

Magnolia invites Jean inside, but he's stuck for a moment in the doorway, awed by the half-packed boxes, the fresh furniture, and the hint of sage she says she lit to purge her ex from her once unhappy home, and it is their first time alone together outside of monitored smoke breaks and eventually Jean moves and one of her hands is at the base of his skull pulling him toward her and the other hand shuts the door and they are lost in the type of rapture they've seen in movies, the click of the lock, leaning against the wall along which they fumble their way to the bedroom, kissing, stripping clothes like responsible adults, and they fuck without an ounce of kink and roll over with eyes open in the evening, think about dinner, about going home or not, they parse through expectations, what regular people, not addicts, would do and they decide while cuddling in the faded sunlight, to not, any longer, wake up alone.

Recovery/Relapse

The videoed interviews were cut to focus on specific narratives and those narratives were loosely grouped into categories such as *Overdose, Withdrawal, Recovery, Relapse,* and in those recorded stories we were all different people, but we found we used drugs in similar ways, practice passed down by word of mouth, and we cringed and understood as we watched the anonymous woman introduced as Magnolia as she reminisced about her once-dealer to whom she'd trade her spit backs for a baggie and how she'd watch as he slurped her backwashed methadone down, from her mouth to the ramekin to dribble over his lips like an opioid kiss, and she'd woken up from a nod once to the two of them holding hands and soon they moved in together till he overdosed, eyes closed, head back, and in the interview she described how she looked him up after year one of sobriety and saw ex-dealer and his new wife holding hands on the beach, and how she lost it, her hand replaced, her house a void.

Recovery

Jean gets a message from Louis who's posted up at the West-inghouse, Ohio McDonald's a couple minutes down the street, a thousand miles and many cigarettes from Hope House, and Jean doesn't even question it, gives Louis his mom's address, imagining a friendly face to brighten the basement gloom Jean's pulled down around himself, a set of hands to transcribe, a pair of ears to bounce ideas off, and it's a sunny day when they embrace at Jean's front door, Louis released from his duties, liberated, until Jean pulls him inside, until Louis picks up temp work at the factory and hunches with Jean in the evenings in the basement where they hear stories that could be their own stories, the words repeated, *overdose, withdrawal, recovery, relapse.*

Recovery/Relapse

The group leader reads, *I listened to their stories and found so many areas where we overlapped—not all the deeds, but the feelings of remorse and hopelessness, page three-forty-four*, and the rubber chicken says buckaw and the noisemakers rattle and squeak, but Jean is hung up on how he hasn't seen Magnolia in a couple weeks, a phone straight to voicemail, no answer at her door, and he wonders if she's slipped, whether or not it's his fault because they fucked once, but their lives are incompatible, and outside, while Jean lights one cigarette off the other, _____ clamps his arm and gives him advice, move on and don't dawdle, she's full of negative vibes, under every skirt a slip, a fall, a spasm of overdose death, but of course Jean won't listen, only walks away, only starts his car and loses _____ in the downtown alleys and heads to Magnolia's where the garden is dying and he bangs on the door until she opens it a bit dope-eyed and he kisses that bloom along her clavicle, says that it's no big deal, trust that it's not a total relapse, that they can help each other cope, and her tears are a storm at sea as she stumbles into him, as they keep stumbling.

Recovery

Throughout our interviews with Jean, we all tried to recover by talking about our past, and though, at first, the stories brought back pain and cravings like last gasps through sand-filled lungs, eventually our narratives lost their charge, not disowned, but claimed, converted into lifelines that connected us, ensured we were no longer alone, commonalities brighter than divisive politics, beyond religion, literature, art, because it was shared trauma and desperation that looped us into the group hug, the oft-embarrassed anthem sung about us, heroes who conquered their pasts.

Relapse

Jean calls _____ the week he and Louis move in with Magnolia, and _____ meets him at McDonald's where the coffee is too hot but Jean lets it burn, lets the burn be penance, and Jean still believes _____ has a fundamental misunderstanding of the difference between sponsor and stalker, but Jean has slipped and is desperate for a friend, so while they scald their mouths with tiny sips, _____ tells Jean that his only hope is to cut ties, that _____ owns a cabin off the beaten path, a lake nearby, and with no one around there will be no influence, and Jean refuses any help this time, so close to the completion of his project, so intent on the idea that folklore holds the opioid epidemic's answers, and he explains how each story about a drug deal gone wrong or a scam that ended in calamity, and each mention of the soma hope of that first heroin shot, makes Jean himself feel like the protagonist, surrounded by friends, encompassed by love, but that it also is like he's a penny on a train's rail, and that each successive wheel wears him smoother, more useless, and he's dulling to a time-dampened shine.

Overdose

In the house that Jean has shared with Magnolia and Louis for only four months, he flicks the tip of the needle, an action entirely ceremonial (every single interviewee flicked the needle at some point in time, *to get the bubbles out*), and while he shoots the stuff into his veins he tries to smile at the woman with the flower tattooed on her throat, but the flower has shriveled as her neck shrinks, as all of her becomes bones in a bag, and even the bag's labels fade, tattoos gone gray, and Jean realizes he needs to uncross his legs before he nods off or he'll cut off the circulation and wake up to a dead foot (this story, told a total of eleven times), but before he can move it all goes black and he comes to with a gasp, a lightning bolt shooting up from his balls because, to save his life, Louis dumps a tray of ice cubes down his pants (a method that, in all fifty-two interviews, is never mentioned) and when that doesn't work, Magnolia squeezes his crotch (severe pain as a cure for overdose mentioned twice), and the pain subsides and he laughs with them, yes, he says, this is really good shit.

Recovery

Our stories told us that our weird histories were not so weird and we laughed along with Louis as he talked in his interview about his friend Jean to the point of tears, and the camera began to shake because Jean was behind it, because he was crying too, or maybe it was a laugh because Louis's story was about stomach cramps that plagued him through withdrawal and the hallucinatory time when Jean convinced him that his problem could be solved by a green tea colonic which he'd heard about from a buddy in lockup, so Jean helped Louis administer the cure with a cut piece of hose in a crusty shower stall, Louis butt naked and Jean soaked with cold sweat, a teapot swiped from kitchen clean-up, a twisted notebook funnel, and what that scene must have looked like to the security guard at two in the morning on his bleary-eyed rounds, and Louis said, *For real, a true friend gives a friend a jailhouse colonic.*

Relapse

Jean will receive his four-year coin and a month later he'll walk out of Magnolia's house, leave her and Louis nodding on the couch, just a backpack slung over one bony shoulder, and all the recordings, transcriptions, legal pads filled with notes, are miles away in his mother's basement, but Jean is out the door and he's an addict, and everything's, once again, fucked, but as he opens the door of _____'s car, he also has hope for another chance at a sober future, hope spurred on by the moment when _____ goes in for half a hug, a sideways lean and clutch that tells Jean everything will be cool, that he's making the right choice, and _____ is so proud of Jean, that he knows when it's time to call for help, tells Jean that _____'s method is foolproof, and _____ holds out his palm, waits for Jean to hand over his coin, and Jean gives up the last four years of his life and once again Jean is a man in his thirties, ashamed and lonely, and he begins to sweat and shake.

Recovery

We didn't know each other, but we'd all shit on the same Hope House pots, all eaten the sawdust breakfast, the pond muck lunch, all dreaded the muggy heat, and at least most of us had holes in our arms, in our feet and wrists, behind the knees, we'd all buckled belts around our biceps, watched scars heal and rooted through them for a vein only to once again get clean, let them scab over, and we'd been silent all those sober years, unable to make our scars disappear, so we hid them until Jean came along with Hope House Grads, with interviews and messages that ripped us all wide open so we could tell our stories and not be blamed for histrionics, for melodrama or rags-to-riches clichés, and, yes, some of us were rich and some of us still struggled, so we started GoFundMes for medical bills and, more than that, we helped each other remember, because it was dangerous to forget.

Withdrawal

Jean won't cry even though they are all gone. Magnolia. Louis. Jean's mom. Even _____ has left. And Jean's also gone, or at least he's only pain. Cramps and restless legs and bowels churning. Sweat and heat and itch. He's not a body anymore, just every bad feeling which includes hopelessness. Which includes despair. Vinegar and feces and puke. A vision of light that jabs angrily through the cracks of _____'s cellar door which Jean knows is padlocked from the outside. Which, for a while, Jean punched as cravings overtook reason. For a time, he pleaded through the door. He made promises, wagered his life against sobriety like he knew he would. Now he pukes up metallic water. The water is siphoned in with a hose poked through the barred window. Jean follows the hose to blinding bright. He's been tricked and lied to, wants nothing to do with AA or its coins. He'll sucker punch _____ and _____'s fool-proof method. Jean only wants to understand his life. Without rubber chickens and higher powers. Without skirts and slips. With folklore. But now it's back to questions.

Recovery

We found each other again, years after Jean disappeared, when his mother released his fieldwork to a producer for a film about Jean's life, so the documentarian phoned us for follow-ups about Hope House and Jean and his work, and we told Jean's story, or at least the little we could puzzle together from anecdotes and fragmented timelines, and we presented these stories to cameras, happy to spread the word about our friend Jean, and when the film was finished we met at the screening and sipped tonics at the reception, dressed fancy (forty-nine of us) or at least in something nice, and we were sober (all but one who turned back to drink after his wife divorced him) and there was Louis, the best friend, who fidgeted with a fresh ninety-day coin, and there was Magnolia, Jean's mysterious lover, also sober, once again, and we were sober with her and we squeezed her hand, and Louis raised a glass, *for Jean*, and we raised our glasses as well.

Recovery

Jean has been at least six different people, as many as fif-ty-two because each narrative of drug abuse is, in a way, his own narrative (e.g. one Jean swallowed spit backs, and another spat them out, five of him boiled needles, thirty-two used bleach), however, this current version of Jean is more unique and he works toward something helpful only for himself and once Jean regains control of his body, and once he's allowed to emerge from the cellar, he begins repairs on _____'s cabin, patches the rowboat, and fishes for dinner and he plants a garden, watches the sunset from a freshly-painted swing on the porch and when _____ finally trusts Jean enough to leave him on his own for a few months, Jean forgets how to talk, then talks to everything and nobody and when _____ visits, Jean asks him *why me*, but _____ just says he's only here to help, so now Jean floats alone in the rowboat and remembers the stories, the narratives and folklore, the phantom pains, mythologies and ceremony, the luck that never let him die, or rather killed one him and sprouted another in its place.

Captain Failure

A Novella

Between trees, a slender woman lifts up the lovely shadow
Of her face, and now she steps into the air, now she is gone
Wholly, into the air.
I stand alone by an elder tree, I do not dare breathe
Or move.
I listen.
The wheat leans back toward its own darkness,
And I lean toward mine.

From "Beginning" by James Wright

Part I: Westinghouse, Ohio

The heart of Ohio had been rubbled before. A landscape lathed by glaciers, bunched into hills and a sprawl of moraines regrown with maple, sycamore, and hemlock only to be stripped again and plowed to farmland, edged with walls of Ice Age granite chucked from the furrows cut in the loam. Then, the buildings of Westinghouse struggled skyward only to stagger through recessions, deindustrialization till the brickwork collapsed. A new landscape of storefronts gone blank, old factories devoured by vines and heavy rains whose runoff sunk to the creek and flowed away.

The creek, Cotter's Run, trickled on through the countryside, branched off to cut up cow pastures, bypassed by bridges, and it searched deeper into the limestone, crumbled the sandstone bluffs into its bed. It cut a floodplain, a field of rich earth covered with slumped trailers and pole barn bunk houses, a central lodge, the compound of The Church of Future Souls which, in time, reroofed itself with moss, graffitied and grown over. It was as if it had been placed in that lush country to pleasure a god who forgot his people, moved on and left his followers to wallow in the mud.

And all these layers of history were splayed beneath a cloudy autumn sky, viewed from a Beechcraft single-prop airplane, flown by two brothers in the dusk of their lives, who shouted at each other over the chopped air, remarked on what was, and what is, and what would soon come. They buzzed fields gone fallow, over swatches of timbered hillside now stubbled. It had all been ruined then left to regrow. All those histories covered up or rendered back to nature once again, but at that moment, evident in a five-minute flight.

ᔑ

In the cockpit, Dunk appraised his brother, Robbie, in his private pilot whites. Half a century from their angsty youth, Dunk's brother had become the type of retiree that waged war on age, armed with black hair dye and a skin care regimen to reduce his smile lines. Dunk could feel his own wrinkles in contrast, flesh leathered from naps in too much California sun, his hair coarse now, a silver-gray, shoulder-length mop. The difference was between Robbie's manufactured sheen and Dunk's own body, hacked by nature. It was chef-prepared dinners and queen-sized beds versus Dunk's dive bars and a buddy's couch.

Robbie looped the plane one more time above the extant cult, the disused compound where the two of them were raised, and Dunk let Robbie drone on about the history of The Church of Future Souls' demise, even though he'd heard all of it before. It was government land now and too expensive for the city to upkeep, left to juvenile delinquents and paranormal investigators, too haunted to inhabit for more than a night. Their parents' trailer was now obscured in a stand of pines. Like Dunk's faith, the commune had faded back to the natural world. Robbie shouted over the engine noise, It wasn't until 1973 when the FBI finally shut that shit down. But the raid was actually two months earlier when they showed up without a warrant. Illegal as shit.

Dunk said, I know, dude.

That was right after you left.

I know.

Right after you ratted us out.

I remember. Fuck.

Robbie straightened out the flight path so the compass pointed north. He said, I haven't seen you in decades, bro. How should I know what you remember?

Dunk shook his head. Come on, dude. I just got here. Give me a break.

He'd arrived at Robbie's with all his belongings in two black trash bags, and, after a mile walk from the bus stop, Robbie'd greeted him at the door and told him to hurry up. They had to boogie.

An hour later they taxied out of Robbie's hangar and Robbie, a couple beers deep, was already lodged in his pas-sive-aggressive bullshit. Dunk stared out the window as they dipped below a cloud until Robbie spoke up: But I forgive you, bro. You know that? Now that you're sober.

Dunk nodded. He was a week out of detox, still suffered the occasional shiver, the restless legs at night. When there was nothing else to think about, he considered his wasted, fucked-up life, cravings for booze or a fat white line. Sixty-five years old and he'd spent most of them focused on escape, and now he was back in his Podunk hometown. Back where it all started. The first place he ever wanted to leave.

Robbie carved the plane upward. He said, So, what's the plan?

Dunk said, I mean, something's gotta come along.

You need to have a plan though.

Dunk said, Yeah, dude. I'll find a job. Back on my feet. He

muttered to himself, I still have some money. But that was only part true. What he had was a crumpled envelope filled with his last thousand dollars and some medical bills he was intent on avoiding. Robbie dipped the nose low to buzz a flock of Canada geese, scattering their V formation across the sky. Dunk bit his lip while his brother laughed. He gnawed the inside of his mouth as the plane rose and fell, swerved through cotton-swab-specked blue sky.

Take me for example, said Robbie, I had a plan, bro. Joined the Air Force. Learned a trade.

I know.

Something to fall back on.

Alright.

You can't just seat-of-your-pants it through life. It's about a plan. Stick to the plan. Invest in the future.

I get it.

Are you sure you get it?

I told you, said Dunk, I fucking get it.

You can't just odd-job your way through life. You can't always expect me to be there to catch you.

Can you lay off for a minute?

The plane juddered through a shock of turbulence which shut Robbie up as he held the course.

After a while, Robbie pointed to the steering wheel between his legs. He said, The yoke. That's what it's called. Left and right—he moved the yoke and the plane turned. Altitude—he pulled back and the nose pitched up.

He demonstrated more maneuvers, jerked Dunk side-to-side, and Dunk's stomach hopped and dropped with the rise and plunge. It reminded Dunk of that day on the commune when Robbie tried to teach him to drive, when they'd taken the old farm truck while the staff held their Forty-Hour Pray-In and Robbie showed off some high-speed drifts around tight corners before he gave Dunk the driver's seat. Dunk was sixteen, old enough to have been a sophomore if the parishioners had believed in sending kids off to school, and Robbie was two years older, well on his way to becoming a parishioner. Robbie said, One day, when you're old enough, you'll need to know how to drive. Maybe they'll task you with transportation. This way you'll be one step ahead. But when Dunk took the county road to the Interstate, clicked the blinker to merge southbound, Robbie freaked and grabbed the wheel. His left foot maneuvered beneath the dash to smash the brake pedal to the floor. Idling on the shoulder, Robbie said, Hell you doing, Dunk? We can't leave. He argued that Mover Roy would whip the shit out of them and where would they even go? What kind of life was out there, beyond faith, unaided by community, family? That was back when Dunk imagined the road flowed one-way toward nirvana, a life outside of rules, beyond scrutiny, no longer surveilled. The Earth, the expanse of it, was somewhere he could disappear. Those tough years when all the hope Dunk owned was an eighteenth birthday, emancipation, a hitchhike to the coast.

The plane fringed the border of Lakeshore where Dunk spent the last ten years employed at Scusi Cellars' Oldtown Winery. He lived in the boss's guesthouse and wasted his cash tips on gritty blow and house Cabernet which he guzzled till his cheeks reddened, till his past was blotted out. He had moved to Oldtown because it was a couple hours' drive north of Westinghouse, and he wanted to be near enough to attend his parents' final hours at Bexley Assisted Living, but far enough away to never visit. Ten years he lived in Scusi's guesthouse and during that time his parents passed away and he forgot about family, Robbie, the cult. What was there for Dunk but the moment, the buzz, the wild ride that was Scusi's wine bar? Until that too was stripped away. The fun had ended when Dunk's heart stopped, when Scusi fired him, when Dunk was forced to make a change. Now, here was Dunk, the prodigal, cleaned up and crashing in his more successful brother's guest room. It was time to face himself, to make amends, forgive, move past his trauma, and restructure his life. That's what his counselor said in detox. But Scusi's slights still raged behind Dunk, the easy way the boss man let him go. Anger potent as a glass of grappa. Dunk couldn't erase the burn.

Lake Erie was a smooth pebble below them, a glass endless eye. Dunk navigated with gestures and shouts and Robbie steered. To the right Dunk could make out the pedestrian walkways between Oldtown's drinking establishments. He scoped the miniature of the pedal wagon bar below. He pictured the vacationers as they tucked back white flights of fruit-forward booze. He said, Does this window go down? Can I loogie out of it?

But the window was sealed, so Dunk dropped imaginary bombs, pulled a lever and the bay doors opened. Nobody saw it coming. Blam! Retribution. Glass shards blown skyward, brickwork scattered, silk-tied sneers turned to gasps. Mayhem. Massacre. Catharsis. Dunk was shocked by his own capacity for violence. Robbie, at first, rolled his eyes.

Along the beach to Scusi's mansion, Dunk's old home now a tiny shack below them, he shouted, Fuck you, Scusi! And he held his disengaged copilot's yoke like a machine gun, strafing the yard as they chased old Scusi out into the street with bullets nipping his heels. Robbie shouted, You done yet? But Dunk wasn't finished with his Fuck you's! Die you bastards!

Robbie latched onto Dunk's shoulder. He shook him.

Nothing changed except Dunk's entire life when his heart stopped at the end of a shift. And a week later, when he asked for sick pay to get him through detox, Scusi had said they should go their separate ways. The guesthouse needed a good remodel and Dunk was, maybe, too old for this. Scusi said, This job. It's like a party. You can't keel over at a party.

So that's a no? Dunk asked.

It was a kick in the pants. A slap in the face.

The fact was that Dunk couldn't hold down a job, a home, for longer than a blip, which hadn't mattered until he was out of options. *So I'm old*, he thought. He had a decade on all the other addicts in detox, the most at risk of breakdown, both body and mind. *Old, confused, set in my ways. At what point*, Dunk had wondered, *is it too late to change?*

Dunk cussed.

Robbie said, Chill, man. Chill. Remember: *He who dwells in anger...*

For real? Dunk said, Quoting Mover Roy for fuckin' real?

It's the truth, man.

It's brainwashing.

It's not all bad, bro.

Robbie toned down the throttle. He said, Take a breath, bro. You want to give it a try? He explained once again that it was an expensive plane, so just a couple minutes, but Dunk held the helm for a quarter hour, banked on the thin air, lost himself in the swoop and sway. It wasn't all bad, but none of it was good. The Mover's words echoed inside Dunk: One truth, one meaning passed on from the celestial savior through Mover Roy's mouth. Beatings if you questioned The Mover, dissenters publicly humiliated, disappeared. Robbie was silent beside him except for sporadic gasps at sudden shifts. All that shared trauma and anger so many years behind and miles below them but it shaped them differently. Opposite ends of the spectrum in almost every way. Dunk yanked back on the yoke and they rose.

〜

They called it a Community, Work Study, Residency, but The Church of Future Souls was a cult. And they called him Leader, Wise One, Elder, but Mover Roy was a scrawny gun-loving pot farmer with a twisted mind, a powerful will, and a couple hundred acolytes. When the FBI ended their investigation, they'd discovered a warehouse-worth of marijuana, a roomful of guns, and seven miles of underground tunnels that led to and from the Big Lodge, connecting outbuildings, bomb shelters, secret egresses into thick woods. There was a stem that jutted off beyond the property, a mainline to the city. The two-mile stretch let out into the basement of the Worlinger Department Store on Westinghouse square, where Dunk's parents helped smuggle Mover Roy's guns and drugs. Dunk and Robbie, in their younger years, stocked the shelves at their parents' store and caught glimpses of the outside world around them through stolen newspapers and magazines.

Both boys were raised in these tunnels, on the several hundred acres of Church land. In their younger years they guided mining carts of pot underground from compound to downtown and loaded it on the Worlinger's trucks, or on warmer days they kicked through the creek, sifted in its gravel for flakes of gold. They memorized psalms in the hay field, prayed their prayers while they tended to the horses, herded the sheep. But as the brothers got older, they disappeared from chores to mole their way through the underground system, the escape route that ended in the boulder-strewn gorge, and there they discovered a secret cave where they taught themselves to roll their own, where they stoned themselves for hours on Mover Roy's dope. Dunk decorated the cave with dried wildflowers and stacked stones, strung chicory garlands on rock altars. One day, when they came across a vein of clay, Robbie shaped a massive water bong, chest high, and once it dried, they ripped themselves stupid.

It was a sin for a parishioner to use the dope they grew. Mover Roy said, Drugs are for the damned. Not the pure. Not the holy.

But it's bullshit, Dunk told Robbie. You can smell it on The Mover. He's a hypocrite. He smokes it too.

Fuck The Mover, Dunk said in the midst of another smoke session. Nothing's stopping us. We could leave.

Robbie told Dunk to shut up. The Mover had a nose for dissenters. He'd sniff them out.

Robbie bent the rules, didn't break them. God, The Mover, they would forgive Dunk and Robbie this pot-doused trespass, but it was heresy to question The Plan. It was a high crime to plot against The Church of Future Souls, to consider defecting. Plus, Robbie said, it's not like you have to believe it. Just act like you do. Look at all this. You want to leave it all behind? You want to be out there? Hunted? Alone?

Anyways, Robbie said, Everyone lives two lives.

I don't, said Dunk.

Robbie shook his head. Took a hit. Passed the bong.

The weed was good. It cleansed Dunk, spun the unanswerable questions off to far corners of the galaxy, and when he returned to work the fields with a significant buzz, there was community with the animals, the Earth, grass tickling his feet, his head in the clouds. In one of the magazines he swiped from the Worlinger was a story about a busload of hippies living wild and free, cruising up and down the West Coast. Fresh air, sea breeze, rock music and weirdos to meet. One head spoke about bare feet in the sand, a communion between Earth and man that felt more holy than toiling per The Mover's supreme will, more sacred than services and hearings and public punishments and tunneling beneath the city to an unspoken end. The

Earth was kinder outside The Church of Future Souls. Maybe even heaven itself.

Dunk had his vial filled with specks of gold, maybe fifty dollars if he pawned it. Beyond that, he had no clue what to expect.

In that cave Dunk ceded to Robbie. Both brothers were beyond convincing and neither knew a scrap about the outside world. He said, I won't tell if you won't. And Robbie bubbled up a hit from the bong, and the brothers smoked themselves Cro-Magnon stupid and were late after the supper bell tolled. Then, a couple days later, they tunneled back and did it again.

⌒

Now deep into adulthood, Robbie had graduated from his makeshift pipe and that cave in the gorge to a finished basement, where the dope haze hung more palpably. Dunk had only been in Westinghouse for a week when he woke from his evening nap to a psych-rock stoner din outside his borrowed bedroom's door. Robbie hadn't mentioned anything about guests or a party, but when Dunk blinked into the den, he choked on a reefer cloud.

Robbie held up the joint, said, Sorry to wake you, bro. But you can't expect us all to suffer.

Dunk bit his tongue, took a seat, picked at the sleep in his eyes while Robbie lectured the group on how to separate business and pleasure. He said it was a balance. Look clean and ride dirty. He said nobody suspected a vial of coke in the pocket of fresh-pressed slacks, and no one would drug test a Windsor knot. Who would guess that Robbie dropped acid monthly and got fucked up on weekends? Robbie said, You just gotta have self-control. Not like this guy. Robbie slapped Dunk's back and Dunk flinched. Robbie said, Just fucking around.

The neighbors sat across from Dunk and his brother on the other end of the horseshoe couch, and they hit the blunt like a last gasp. Dunk figured they were in their twenties, a poet and a musician whose names didn't stick, and the Poet's girlfriend, Mara, perched on the sofa arm, tap-dancing thin fingers across the phone screen under a tent of straight black hair. Dunk wondered if maybe it was the secondhand inhalation that had him drawing blanks on names, but maybe it was just the fact that the neighbor dudes were too boring to make much of an impression. They were low-level dealers who bought designer drugs off the dark web and they spent most of that first hour talking about the good shit they could score on the low. It was easy to remember Mara though, the vowel sounds of her name on repeat in his mind. There was an intelligence in her silence, whole diatribes left unsaid for the sake of peace. She lorded over the scene. He glanced at her while he watched basketball players scatter from one backboard to the other on Robbie's muted big screen.

Both the Musician and the Poet wore paint-splattered clothes, jeans with holes in the knees, the Poet with Larry Fine's scraggle of curls while the Musician's White dude dreads hung ratty below his shoulders. Mara was taller, thin, but wrapped in her own yogic ball. Robbie zoned out beside Dunk, like he was becoming one with the couch. *Phish: Live in Brooklyn* spun heady jams on the turntable. Another difference between the two brothers: Dunk had once followed the Dead. It was the blur of smoke around them. The all-too-familiar litter of beer cans, the pop and hiss of them opening. Drool pooled in Dunk's mouth. The record was clicking at the end of its run as the neighbors talked about the acid they were about to take.

The Musician said, Fuck man, just wait till it hits you—he pinched his thumb and forefinger together—primo.

The Poet snapped his fingers, said, Hey Mara, you got the orange juice, right?

Mara glared at him and went back to her phone.

The Poet said, Jesus Christ, Mara. It was right there on the table.

Mara ignored him.

The Poet said, Vitamin C, babe. Fucking important.

Dunk sat up out of his craving, annoyed. He said, Anyone care if I put on a record?

They all looked at him, but didn't respond.

Dunk spun Flower Travellin' Band, Yuya Uchida fucking wailing, that signature squawk of guitar, and Dunk couldn't help but patter out the drums on his thigh, bounce his upper body like an impatient child. He wanted to lift the tension, to meet them in their stoner zone. He wanted to get caught up in the sound as if maybe the music would cure his craving, level him out. The others tapped their feet, lost to the haze of a timeless satori. Mara didn't move, but Dunk sensed a softening. There was no longer anything between the five of them but the rhythm and Joe Yamanaka's howled *Freedom! Freedom!* Who needs weed when you have that song?

He sank into the music. He daydreamed of shows in the past.

The Poet said, You gonna hit that?

A joint had appeared in Dunk's hand, and it was making a beeline for his mouth.

He looked down at the roach, ember dying. It was so normal, a piece of his anatomy, now reduced to a phantom limb.

Robbie reached over and slapped the joint out of Dunk's hand.

The needle rode the label.

Robbie said, Get yourself to-fucking-gether, Dunk. No drugs or you're back out on the street.

∽

Dunk counted his breaths outside to cool down. He'd made it seven days, but still didn't have a job, hardly even had the energy to look for one. Sobriety was hard enough without his brother reminding him of his failure. He could gather his bags, take his cash, hitch rides westward, find a place to stay. He didn't know phone numbers, but he knew people. Big Hawk and his winery in Northern California, Dougie at his Oregon grow op. If they were still there. If they could be cool with Dunk's newfound sobriety. All his friends were heavy drinkers or users, and Dunk was beginning to understand the rift his abstinence created. He needed to lay off the shit to survive, but was survival worth it if you were all alone?

The asphalt driveway was as black as the overcast Midwest sky. He stilled himself into meditation and the breeze combed through his hair, wrapped him up in the Universe's warmth. He was centered, a puppet buzzed to life by an electric sky. All he had to do was wait for a sign, for the Universe to tweak a string into perfect pitch. When he opened his eyes Mara stood in front of him, hit a personal pinner joint. She said, I wasn't sure if you were having a heart attack there or what.

Dunk drew a chuckle out of his self-pity. Been there. Done that, he said.

She had a soft voice, and low, like a smoker but if cigarettes were coated in maple syrup instead of menthol. She said, No offense cause he's your brother and all, but those guys are a bunch of dicks. She explained that they'd all taken their acid, but her boyfriend was worried the hit would react with her medication, so they cut her out. It was really revenge over the forgotten orange juice, she knew, but there was nothing to be done. She offered Dunk the joint.

Dunk waved his hand, shook his head. He said, Sorry, dude. I really am in recovery.

Mara toked. She took a bunch of little puffs and then exhaled a thin stream out the corner of her mouth. She said, No worries. More for me. She smoked again. She said, I'm not even sure why I do it anymore. Maybe just because it makes things more interesting, different.

Dunk nodded. He understood. He fumbled his hands in his pockets looking for something to say.

Mara explained that she had her own apartment downtown, eight months left on the lease till she moved in with her boyfriend and the Musician, but tonight she wondered whether she should hit the road instead, never come back because her boyfriend just, what? Expected her to, like, sit there and watch him trip or something, like she didn't have a life?

She said, Sorry. I'm oversharing. I'm stoned.

She said, I'm not that interesting.

No, Dunk said, You're fine. Just be careful, is all. Don't want to end up like me.

A storm hovered over them, waiting to break. Dunk could smell it, one of those post-summer fronts that barrels through, downpours, and then fades to stillness. There was a question of lightning on the horizon. Mara killed the joint and scrubbed it out with her sandal. She said, Want to go for a ride?

༄

Mara drove like she wanted to die, a tallboy in the cup holder, yet another joint in her hand. She took corners so fast Dunk had to grab the oh-shit handle so he wouldn't tip into her lap. Then the rain came, pebble-sized and howitzer heavy, loud as the growls of thunder, and there was lightning that cut cracks in the sky. They took a right on Elmer Road just before the old compound and Dunk became lost as Mara cut the car down a gravel path. Soon they were walled in by trees on one side, steep granite on the other, and Dunk was snatched back by memory, once again visiting his stoner cave with Robbie.

He didn't want to remember, but without a buzz he couldn't stop the mental images. He was a kid again, Robbie a young adult, and Dunk recalled that the rain wasn't so heavy that evening. He remembered the mouth of the cave, the glow and flicker of fire as he and Robbie crept up the ridge. And then they saw the man, Protector Benjamin, who fed the flames with Dunk's stolen newspapers and magazines, Dunk's access to the world, incinerated, vanished. The protector spotted them, called out their names, told them to come closer and repent. Dunk didn't know then, would probably never fully understand, how he found, in his hand, a fist-sized rock. He floated toward the protector in a cloud of rage. All those images and articles, each a connection to the outside world, the real world, every glossy hope flaked to ash in the flame. The protector said something and Dunk swung the stone, a crack much duller than thunder as the rock connected with Benjamin's head.

Dunk remembered he apologized, kept apologizing to Robbie, but there was no absolution. Robbie said, We're fucked, man. We're fucked. Get away from me.

Robbie continued swearing as Dunk backed out of the cave, watched everything he once loved destroyed. Robbie said, What the fuck, Dunk? What have you done? He repeated himself, stumbling past a weak-kneed Dunk. I have to tell them, Dunk. Maybe it won't be that bad.

Dunk emerged from the cloud to a needle-sharp focus. He said, Robbie! This is it. We have to run.

Robbie didn't answer. He tripped his way down the ravine toward home.

Alone, Dunk considered what to do. He'd often pondered

the pay phone in front of the Worlinger, but never punched in a number. The tunnels, empty at this hour, would take him there. His feet moved on their own volition, each step driven by adrenaline, by the right thing to do. He'd never touched the phone, but he'd read the sign beside it that directed him to poke the numbers 911 for emergency. He listened to the faraway voice come clear through the wires. When they asked him questions, he answered honestly, locating the bales of pot, the stashes of guns. The voice on the line said, What is your name? He stopped responding. When the voice asked him to stay where he was and wait for assistance, he ran.

Dunk shook off these memories, returned to Mara's car. He said, You know, me and Robbie were part of that cult, right? The Church of Future Souls.

Mara said, Holy shit, man! She couldn't hide her grin. She said, I mean, that place is like a legend. I saw the documentary.

Dunk said, It was sort of my fault they got busted.

It was an anonymous tip, right? That's what they said.

Yeah, he said, My tip. If I hadn't, they might still be there. No shoot-out. No arrests.

So, you're like some kind of fucking hero or something. Badass.

Doesn't feel badass, Dunk said, All I did was run away.

Mara hit her joint, hotboxed the car. Take the compliment. You were smart enough to survive.

Zeppelin's *When the Levee Breaks* crackled on the Volvo Wagon's radio, just underneath the rain's constant roar. Lightning up ahead, followed by a roll of thunder. Mara cranked down the window and ejected the spliff. A gust shuddered through and Dunk could hear something rattle. Mara said, Nothing like a Midwest storm.

They bent the Volvo along the black-snake pavement. The trees flanked them, flashed into focus then vanished behind a wall of dark. Mara said, But I guess I don't know any other kind of storm, which is kinda sad.

Dunk wanted to change the tone. He said, Speaking of storms.

He told the story of when he'd toured the South with his buddy's band, the Crusty Blues, how he roadied and consumed a truckload of drugs, and then, in Louisiana, they drove through the wreckage of a hurricane. Piles of splintered timber, heaps of trash. He had weathered tornadoes in Oklahoma, fires in Cali. He'd seen all kinds of destruction and the rebirth that came from it, months, years, decades later.

Mara said, That's what I mean. I'm wasting my life. I haven't seen shit.

Dunk said, I'm sure it's not a waste. You have friends, a place to stay, a car.

Mara rolled her eyes, chugged her beer while she listed the faults of her English degree from the branch campus where she met the Poet. In the local scene, the Poet was a big deal, but, Mara said, He doesn't really write, hasn't made anything new in years. I mean, he's hot shit for Westinghouse, Ohio, but what about the rest of the world? And what does an English degree even mean? Westinghouse is so insular. The whole town's a cult. Well, I mean, obviously it's not a cult. You were in a cult. I'm rambling. Damn.

Mara swerved around a fallen branch and Dunk pushed both feet into the imaginary brakes. The rain rushed them. White noise. Old wipers burped against glass.

Dunk said, I mean, I hate to be a downer, dude, but all that traveling, that chasing the American Dream shit. It's cool for a little while, but then you wake up one day and you've got nothing. There's something to be said for making the best of where you are.

Mara said, Fuck, dude. Don't ruin it.

She laughed.

Her phone lit up in the cupholder.

The radio played "Long Cool Woman in a Black Dress," muffled beneath the engine hum and the rain rattle.

The thunder boomed and cracked.

They saw the barn fire as soon as they crested the hill. A glow at first in the waterlogged distance, becoming brighter. It revealed both sides of the road, backlit apple-orchard rows in the yellow foreground. The rain had slowed enough that, once Mara stopped on the berm, they could watch the red dragons leap out and up from the hay loft. Shadowy figures stood around the inferno, doing nothing. There was nothing to be done. Both Dunk and Mara cussed in awe and Dunk noticed a tear dripping down Mara's cheek, but what was he supposed to do? He wasn't a father figure. He couldn't wipe it away. He wasn't much more than a spectator, a rubbernecker too trapped to help.

Mara said, What can we do?

Dunk thought about this as the sirens blared behind them and the fire truck honked. Mara's phone lit up again, but she didn't even look this time. It vibrated in the cupholder. She turned to Dunk and smiled. She said, Welcome to the Mid-fucking-west. As if he hadn't already been there, done that.

～

It was a cult, a full-blown brainwashing, death-pact-signing, crucify-threatening cult, and after Dunk left The Church of Future souls for the infinite stretches of Western roads, he still struggled with his inculcation for the next forty years. He tried to recover.

In Northern California, when Dunk was in his early twenties, fresh to the free world with all its drugs and booze and communes and delicious colorful psychedelic music, he fell in love with Blue Fawn, spent a month living in her tee-pee. She wasn't Native American, just some White chick from Wisconsin. But everyone from the Midwest believed a small percentage of them was related to some tribe or other, and Blue Fawn deemed herself an ancient spirit and dressed in animal hides, stuck feathers in her hair. She'd left a psychiatric prac-tice to work the collective grow operation in NorCal, and she counseled Dunk in the evening as they cuddled after sex. She would tell him truths about the world, that capitalism's goal was to crush the poor, that god was not singular but all of nature, a conglomerate oversoul. Things that Dunk felt he'd already known, deep down, all his life. She taught him about basic things like high school, boyfriends and girlfriends, that the real reason people went to football games was to be seen, to flirt, to make out under the bleachers. She taught him yoga, played sitar by the fire while the other hippies danced and sang. She told him to let it out and he did, the whippings he witnessed, the memorization of rote verses, the time, as a child, when his father tied him Abraham-style to a pyre on the edge of a cliff. It was a test. Mover Roy showed up before the kindling was lit and saved Dunk from his pious progenitor. He told those stories until they lost their charge, but his guilt still lingered, an unease with which he approached his past. He didn't tell Blue Fawn about the rock he wielded against the protector, about the phone call that led to a shootout and a hundred arrests.

Blue Fawn would pass Dunk a joint after his confessions and say, You've done nothing wrong. Let it go. Forget.

And he did forget. Most of it. He wandered through life, bounced off dead-ends. Then his counselor at the detox, a middle-aged washed-up Jungian who claimed he had worked on the Manson case, dredged it all back up again. The Jungian didn't believe in *brainwashing*. A person couldn't be convinced to believe, only threatened to adapt to the ritual, and Dunk's supposed trauma, his guilt, was nothing more than a relic of his past actions in conflict with his current beliefs. He felt bad because he no longer believed in the cult even though he followed it. This led to a mental schism. Hypocrisy. But Dunk was fine now. He should be true to himself, get over it.

He tried to get over it, but then he returned to Westinghouse and it all piled on top of him.

ᓄ

The morning after the barn fire, Dunk found a note from Robbie by the coffee pot. His brother had early business at the hangar, but wanted to have dinner. It said, *The Dog's Leg. Tonight. 6 p.m. sharp.*

Dunk crumpled the note and pitched it. He picked up the envelope of money he'd left for Robbie and shuffled through the cash, not a dollar short of the five hundred bucks he'd offered for his stay. Robbie didn't care about Dunk's money, didn't need it. Dunk pulled out a fifty and hit the streets.

Sunshine bloomed around him, glistened on the wet from last night's storm. Robbie's neighborhood was filled with rehabbed early twentieth-century relics, immaculate homes with manicured lawns, sparse gardens and short ornate fences, neighborhood watch signs. Not Dunk's kind of place. The porches were empty, but Beamers and Benzes were parked outside their garages. Then he turned onto Fourth Street and the neighborhood transitioned abruptly into ragged rentals with dirt yards and dog chains pinned to the center of worn-to-mud circles. Windows were blacked out by bedsheets. Paint peeled from walls. The old corner store was boarded up, the one Dunk once walked to on his break from the Worlinger to buy underage bottles of Wild Irish Rose. But the people were out. Lawn mowers buzzed. Humans passed blunts beneath the shadows of awnings and overhangs. While Robbie and his friends kept their secrets behind closed doors, this neighborhood was laid bare to the world. A diapered child smeared mud on his face like warpaint. It was busy, honest, laid-back noise.

And then the houses became abandoned buildings. Then downtown sprouted up, a beetle-eaten garden. Dunk wasn't clueless anymore. He'd heard about people rehabbing downtowns, and as he passed through the heart of Westinghouse, he looked in the windows of craft stores and a dance academy, brewpubs and a taco joint. Small-town Ohio grasping at big city trends and tweaking them to fit the thrifty locale. He stopped by the bookstore to browse. There were posters up for author events. He noted a folk singer on Sunday afternoon, book clubs and poetry readings. Sophisticated, but still clinging to that provincial Rust Belt grit. One poet went by the name of Barnstorm Smith. The book club was reading about the opioid epidemic.

Dunk scanned the shelf of local authors, felt the AC chill his damp underarms. A young sweaty White dude dressed in a cardigan like an ersatz professor browsed through fantasy. A Black woman with purple-tipped dreads and a handmade dress shuffled through collections of poetry. He pulled down a book of Westinghouse legends and skimmed it, found stories of Mary Jane's Grave and the one about the Ladies of the Night whose souls faded to ghost lights in the back-alley windows. He began reading about The Church of Future Souls, how parishioners' spirits lurked in the abandoned Worlinger Building waiting to kidnap wayward strangers and suck their blood. Dunk closed the book and shoved it back on the shelf. There was no truth to the bloodsucking. The Mover's claim was to save the Earth, not drain it. To purify the population, not consume them. But then again, Dunk thought, how funny would it be if the parishioners' souls were confined to ghosthood, to haunting, rather than free to roam in the Ever After? What perfect irony. He walked out, didn't even look up when the bookstore lady waved.

⌒

Mara was behind the counter at the Coffee Underground, the old Cruisin' Diner stripped down to its wood floor, ceilings reverted to original stamped tin and run with exposed pipes. IKEA furniture. Corrugated walls. She was busy with a customer, leaning all the way across the steel countertop to trace his palms. Dunk watched her work out the young man's future, the young man blushing under her gaze. She told him something that made him snatch his arm back and as she leaned away, Mara looked over at Dunk. She said, It's you!

Dunk could envision the energy that pinged off Mara, the concentric waves of goodness, of old soul wisdom. He said, I thought I might find you here.

Mara stepped up to the register and said, I'm so sorry about last night. I was, like, super stoned. I honestly don't remember much after we got back.

Dunk said, I hope your boyfriend isn't too pissed.

She waved her hand. I can handle it. He's recording the rest of the month. When he gets in the studio, he just, like, disappears. Nice to have a bit of time to myself.

There were machines that whirred, coffee grinders with different grit settings, nothing like the original downtown diner with Folgers, the gray-stained pot, the griddle burning home fries and omelets. It was a fine replacement though, a rich-earth, robust smell. Dunk watched Mara dribble a pot of hot water into the filter, and the drip plopped into his cup. Mara was focused. It took some time. She said, Do you want a reading?

Dunk smiled, put his hand in both of hers.

She said, What are you hoping to learn?

Dunk told her he was on the job hunt today, and Mara traced the lines through his hands like she was following mapped highways to a known destination. Her fingers stopped. She scowled. She said, Good news! You will find more than a job, more than a career.

Dunk said, What?

She said, Your destiny, maybe? Who knows?

But what about my lifeline? What about my life?

Mara pulled away and went back to pouring coffee. Sorry, she said, I only see what I see.

Dunk said, I bet I'll end up a bartender at the Lantern or something.

Mara halted her pour. The Lantern?

He described the old dive bar, nestled between the steel mill and the highway.

She said, Steel mill? That's been gone forever, since I was a kid. You'll probably be surprised how much everything's changed. She poured and Dunk pondered. He wanted to say something to keep her talking. Talk was so easy last night, would always be even easier with a buzz on, but this sober momentum waned.

She said, Only other thing I can tell you is don't bother looking for jobs at a bar. You deserve better than that. And aren't you sober anyways?

She put down the pot and waited for the last drips to top off the cup.

You're right, he said. But how do you know I'm better than that?

Your hand, Mara said.

Mara nudged the paper cup toward Dunk and he capped it before changing the subject. She went on to explain that there couldn't have been a worse time to look for a job. A movie was about to be filmed in town, a sort of fictionalized action film about the cult. It was supposed to be somewhat historically accurate, though, and they'd rented out the coffee shop to turn it back into the Cruisin' Diner for the filming, so she'd be out of a job as well. The whole town would be put on pause, converted back to the seventies-era facade. There was a call out for vintage cars. Extras would dress in paisley and tie-dye and bell-bottom jeans. She said, There was this whole protest outside of city council for like a week to keep those LA assholes away, but our council caved, sold out. She said, It's not like they haven't done it before.

Dunk sipped his coffee as he walked the final half mile to the temp agency, but Mara was right. The building was empty, a closed sign on the door. He kept walking, crossed the tracks where the old factories were nothing but fenced-in slabs of concrete, Do Not Enter signs, weeds breaking through cement. As Mara had premonitioned, nothing was open. Everything had changed. Dunk had time to kill and booze and drugs were no longer part of the plan.

What did sober people do here besides meetings, church, gallons of coffee?

On his way back to Robbie's, he passed a total of five dive bars, plenty of trap houses, dealers on the street. Since his heart attack at Scusi's and the detox that followed, life had slowed to a trickle, a drudge, but it was better than a lopsided lilt or the bravado-packed gusto with which he once bombarded his customers. There was a time when drugs and booze were fun, but Scusi was right: The fun was over. The pleasure long ago deadened. And even though the past he'd blocked out for so many years now nipped at his heels, he wasn't going to die high. Not drunk or sad or alone.

The Dog Leg Tavern overlooked the ninth hole green at the Lilting Hills Golf Course. In his youth, Dunk would sometimes sneak out of his mom and dad's trailer at night and hustle across the highway to stick his feet in the Lilting Hills sand traps, pretending he was on the beach. He had torn this ad out of one of the Worlinger's magazines. It was women in bikinis holding surfboards and a ripped dude leaning out of a battered truck. It was sexy, which was a delicious sin. But beyond that, there was the ocean, that sense of elsewhere and other, a promise that Dunk found more fulfilling than Mover Roy's afterlife. That was back when he'd had it with religion, with its nearsightedness, strict rules, harsh punishments. That was when he was a teen, before he took off for good. But it wasn't for good, because he was back, peering over the swanky hostess's shoulder to catch sight of Robbie. Back where he started, only now he belonged there even less.

They had to sit at the bar because Dunk hadn't worn a tie, and Robbie ordered himself a scotch, rocks, and told Dunk to get whatever. When the waiter clunked Dunk's water in front of him, he could see it was sparkling. He waited for Robbie to start.

Robbie didn't look up. He said, When I told you the Dog Leg, I thought you'd, you know, maybe dress up a little. At least wash your clothes. I have a washer and dryer you can use. Maybe I forgot to mention that.

Dunk tested his soda water, and it was good to feel the bubbles prickle down his throat.

Robbie went on, But whatever, you're my brother. You're family and family is the source of all forgiveness. He slugged his scotch.

Really? Dunk said, You're quoting Mover Roy?

Robbie waved the question off. Would you get over your-self, Dunk? It's my truth. Family's important. The point is, we sit at the bar. No problem. Whatever you want. I'll pay. Not that there was a question about that.

Dunk swallowed. Thank you. He could picture those same words spilling from the mouth of Mover Roy. Even after death, the man invaded Dunk's mind.

Robbie shot the last of his scotch and ordered a second. He said, You know, the thing is, this is hard on me. I work nonstop. I get my wings. I visit our parents, *our* family. I pay for their home. And all the while my younger brother sows his fucking oats. And who bails him out when he's killing himself? Me. But, I mean, it's no big deal. I take care of family. I work my way to the top.

Dunk gulped more water. He said, Yeah, Robbie. I'm proud of you.

But Robbie held up his hand. He said, I'm not looking for fucking accolades. I'm just saying, if you want something you got to go out and get it and you can't get all hung up on the past. Stop using it as an excuse.

Dunk drank till the ice clunked into his nose. Neither brother looked at the other. They bent over the menu without really reading. Dunk didn't see any prices which meant that it was far above his budget. French and Spanish words speckled the descriptions.

After another drink Robbie said, I brought you out here to tell you something.

What Robbie'd wanted to do was give Dunk an eviction notice, but he tried to put it kinder than that. The film crew had offered Robbie ten thousand dollars to use his house during the month of shooting. The director or some other bigwig would be staying there and Robbie would be moving in with his girlfriend, Mimi, a widow, a few years older than him, and,

Robbie mentioned, she was loaded. She lived in Westinghouse Woods, a neighborhood with a gatehouse blocking the private drive. Robbie slipped around Dunk's questions. No, he wasn't just in it for the money. Yes, they loved each other. No, it wasn't for the sex. Robbie said, We talk. We like the same art. I'm sophisticated, Dunk. It's not all whammy bars and distortion like you. We go to the opera. We have a lot in common.

Dunk said, So, where do I go? Also: Where is the nearest opera hall?

That's the thing, Robbie said, Mimi's not really comfortable with having a, you know, drug addict around. She's on all these pills, see, and, well, you understand?

Dunk understood his crimes, his harm, the trust he'd have to rebuild, but it still rankled.

Then it only hurt.

Dunk nodded.

Robbie shook his head. He said, You need to look at the big picture, bro. Maybe this is the kick in the ass you need.

Dunk said, Do you know of a cheap hotel?

Robbie scoffed. He said, You make no sense. But I'm not here to explain economics to you. Do what you need to. Now, I'm willing to give you back that money you tried to pay me for rent. You'll need it more than me.

Dunk focused on his soda water. The bubbles danced each time he jostled the glass, their pattern, seemingly random, but defined by the universe, by the natural law of the Earth that makes chemical meet with chemical. And all the coincidence of Dunk's near-death experience, how it guided him to sobriety and led him back to this place he once called home, it wasn't some cosmic accident. He could fight or he could trust the flow, drift with it. See where he would eventually go. All these forces shook the glass and Dunk hoped not to spill over, fizz out.

Robbie said, You got it, bro?

Huh? Right, dude. Dunk nodded. He drank deeply.

They'll be here in one week, said Robbie. You sure you're good? I mean, I feel like I need to be stern, but you're also family.

Right on, right on.

And no hard feelings, Dunk. Cool, bro?

Dunk said, Yeah, *bro*. Whatever. It's cool.

⌇

Within forty-eight hours the city was transformed into a modern idea of what it once was, a plywood facsimile of 1970s storefronts, actors roaming the streets, old cars painted with flowers and peace signs.

Fourth Street was cordoned off to one lane, and Dunk sipped his coffee and watched as people swarmed in and out of the throng that buoyed three windowless trailers parked on the street. Movie folk with their mob of rabid fans. Cops nudged people along the sidewalks and out of the backed-up traffic. Dunk crossed to the far side of the street, slunk along behind the hubbub when he heard his name and stopped.

He heard it again, a voice from the maw, and then he saw her, Mara, tiptoeing taller than the rest of the crowd, waving her hand as she edged her way out. She crossed the street and ducked under the police tape. She asked, What are you doing here?

Dunk shrugged.

Mara explained that the actors had arrived last night and now, rumor had it, they were primping in their trailers. My brother, Mara said, He's a huge fan of Ron Crusher. You know, the wrestler guy. He's like the lead in the movie. Rambo-type shit. She rolled her eyes. Anyways, I figured I'd give my bro a ride since he can't drive.

Dunk said, Right on. I'm just walking home from another glorious day of failed job searching

Mara pouted. She apologized, said she really didn't know how to read palms. She was just making it up. Dunk wanted to tell her to stop saying she was sorry, that none of this was her fault. Probably just leftover karma. He'd earned it. But then the crowd grew louder, bunched forward. Bodies swayed.

Mara said, Shit! That's him. I gotta go.

She said, Wait for me.

༈

Dunk waited for Mara until his coffee was cold, but before she could get Crusher's signature, the actor was hustled and folded into a waiting Escalade. Mara's brother pouted as they walked to Mara's Volvo, and Mara promised to cheer him up as they headed out of the city.

Mara said, Jake, dude, show Dunk your kites.

Jake held up a handmade diamond of fabric. It wasn't anything like the usual Walmart junk people hiked up a hundred feet in the air with thread. These were dowel rods hand-sewn to printed canvas, strung with tassels and twine. Jake said, The first one was just a project for art class, but I became enamored, the contours, recalibrating for the drag. Not just the object, but the way it moves. This is art.

Jake mentioned wind speed and aerodynamics, formulas and functions that were beyond Dunk. That Dunk marveled in. He'd never controlled a kite, only ever just tossed them up there and let them cruise.

Dunk was so caught up in Jake's lecture that he didn't notice where they were going until Mara turned down the driveway to

The Church of Future Souls. The car bumped over the busted asphalt toward the main lodge which was big as ever but now vines climbed the wall joists, and doors and windows were boarded-over, graffitied. A brown-stained mattress crumpled against one wall and the blank face of the building, once a Noah's Ark mural with all the animals, was only sharded stucco, the spray-painted slogan: *Ellie S. is a whore.*

Mara said, Oh my god. I didn't even think, man. Is this cool?

Dunk realized she was speaking to him. Of course it was cool. It was nothing. It wasn't his fault. He was over it.

They had to wade through belly-high grass spotted with patches of multiflora rose that pulled on his pants, on Mara's dress. The once-hand-cut grass now grew up to hide trash bags, old shucked clothes, bald tires. They came upon a trampled-down clearing, a fire pit in the middle and a tractor path headed back to the road. Jake had already hoisted his kite and played the string out one slow loop at a time. His was littered with kanji beyond Dunk's comprehension, and it decreased in font size till the symbols were only a speck in the sky. They got Mara's kite up next. Dunk held it as she ran and then tossed the dragon in the air. Mara kicked off her sandals and a breeze blew her, whooshed her hair all wild around her face, and for a minute Dunk felt something like longing for the way she moved so freely in the shadow of the church. Innocent and unhindered. A jealousy he sucked back down into himself. They were both their own entities with their own struggles. They belonged to the Earth. He balanced his kite on his fingertips and sprinted until, for a moment, he flew too, his legs lifted from the ground, the kite piercing the blue. Their lines tying their kites to the earth, their bodies to the fish-scale-clouded sky.

Mara said, So, you sure you're cool with this? I know they did some traumatic shit.

Dunk said, I'm over it. It was like fifty years ago.

She said, You don't have to answer if you don't want, but did they *really*, like, hang people on crosses and put crowns of thorns on their heads?

Every Easter.

And they actually, like, made you read the bible and if you fucked up they would lock you up underground?

Yes.

So, why didn't more people leave? What kept you?

Dunk wanted to say it was family, but it wasn't just that. It was safety that held them, a fear of what harm existed outside the fold. They shared everything, knew each other's secret wants. It was all he ever knew, and he knew it better than if it had been tattooed in the crevices of his mind. The cult was him as much as it was all its other members. Until it wasn't. Until the outside world filtered in with its lack of certainty, its magic, its questions.

He said, I mean, the whole thing's pretty hard to explain.

Mara said, You got something—she tapped a finger against her upper lip.

Dunk wiped at his nostril and his finger came away with a touch of blood. A repercussion of years insufflated, ripped into capillaries, He rubbed the blood on his shirt sleeve. Turned away.

He said, Just a tiny nose bleed.

He tipped his head back till it stopped, watched fabric flick to specks in the wind.

There was the divine swish of blown grass, the majestic sway of branches. There was a holy hush in which all worry slipped away.

The hush was cut by the motorized growl of truck engines, the crunch of gravel followed by the thump of tires along the tractor path. Jake reeled in his kite, looked around nervously, and Dunk and Mara watched the two blacked-out Escalades jostle toward them through the field and stop at the edge of the clearing.

Caricatures of private security emerged, black suits, sunglasses, and coiled wires dangling from their ears. Dunk brought in his kite as well, but Mara turned her back to the Cadillacs as if she hadn't even noticed them, let out a bit more string, shrugged her shoulders dramatically. She said, We're allowed to be here.

Then, a behemoth of a man, seven feet tall, the arms of his jacket as big around as Dunk's thigh, stepped down, made the SUV bounce as it was relieved of his weight. Mara looked, then tried to look away, then tried to look casual while she visibly reddened. Jake gaped. He stilled against the wind. He whispered, Holy shit! It's Crusher.

They met the stars halfway, kids confronted by hardass adults. Dunk noticed the crumpled foliage the SUVs had paraded through, the careless trample of whatever stood in their way.

Following Ron Crusher was a scrawny and animated man. He swung his arms while he walked, looked like a prematurely aging child with a purple jacket and florid scarf, yellow-tinted shades which he removed with a flourish before he shoved them into his pocket. He said, I really do hate to *do* this to you because it *does* look like such fun, but we have a lot of important work ahead and this is private property.

Dunk said, Oh. Is it?

As if she didn't know, Mara said, And who the hell are you?

Ron Crusher stepped forward. He stretched out his hand. You know who I am, right? From the Grip trilogy?

Mara shook her head, lips pursed like a pissed child.

He said, Ron Crusher. The Crusher. I look different without the cape and the mask and all that.

Mara still pretended, glared.

Jake still gaped.

Crusher's hand still jutted out and Mara still ignored it as she said, Oh, so you're like the guy who was supposed to be signing autographs but took off before he was done.

Crusher's hand fell to his side.

The small man moved in front of them, said, Mick Jonathan, director. He dipped a couple inches in a half-assed curtsy. He said, And we need to get this place ready for the shoot, so, again. I apologize, but. Mick Jonathan wished them away with a wave of his hand.

Mara glared at the man, stepped forward, face-to-face. She said, As if you have any right to be here. Just traipse into town. Dunk was born here, raised right here, and you're kicking him out? She pointed back at Dunk.

Dunk shook his head.

Mick Jonathan stopped. He looked Dunk up and down, measured him. He said, You lived here?

Dunk nodded. But it's not a big deal. We can leave. It's cool, dude.

You mean, Mick said, You were in the cult?

Dunk nodded.

Mara said, We don't have to leave, Dunk.

Mick Jonathan said, What luck!

Mara said, You don't even, like, live here. Just turn around and drive off back to your fancy houses and shit.

Mick Jonathan gave her a fake smile. He reached inside his jacket and pulled out his card. He said, Dunk, is that right? How would you like to make some money?

Dunk took the card. Questions sprouted and then were buried under nerves. His face flushed.

Mara said, I don't think he's interested.

Dunk said, I'm sorry. I'm a bit confused.

Mick Jonathan said, I'm offering you a job. I need authenticity to sell this film. You, sir, could bring that authenticity. Fact checking. Consulting. Call it what you want. Not much work but big big bucks.

Mick turned to Mara and said, I'm really sorry, but we just need a month tops and then you can fly your kites wherever the hell you please.

Ron Crusher grunted.

Mick said, And Ron will sign all the autographs you want. Mick waved to one of the guards who ducked back into the SUV. Mick said, So what do you think? Trailer number two. Tomorrow. Noon.

Dunk wasn't sure.

Think about it. And by the way, you have a little something right here. Mick touched his upper lip.

Part II: Ron Crusher in *Revenge on The Cult of Future Souls*

They first shot the action scenes from the beginning of Act III.

The grenade plunked along the concrete and teetered at Protector Jack Tokerson's feet, and for a moment, everyone was still, silent. Ron Crusher, ex-cult-member, bloodied but armed for vengeance, faced Tokerson and his squad of protectors, all of whom stood open-mouthed, eyes on the grenade. Ron smiled, said, Shove that up your righteous ass!

The explosive roared. The pulley systems ripped the cultists away from the eruption and toward the bundles of fake pot leaves.

The smoke dissipated.

Mick Jonathon shouted, Cut! Well done!

Dunk's ears rang, seated next to Mick in their director's chairs. As the crew dribbled blood spatter around the blown-apart bodies to prepare for the next shot, he felt the cruller from the breakfast spread curl in his stomach.

Mick slapped Dunk's back. What do you think? It's good, yeah? Anything we missed?

Yeah, said Dunk. Good. He swallowed his food back down. It's just a lot gorier than I expected.

Mick laughed. That's the point! This is Ron Crusher we're talking about here. Not Ron *gentle nudger*. The cult is evil and for Ron's character it's like catharsis, purging his past one explosion at a time. You hear that, Ron? Maybe you should come over here for these notes. You see, this evil cult tried to ruin Ron's childhood, tried to annihilate his individuality, blow apart, like figuratively, any chance at a normal life. Now Crusher is returning the favor. Blood for blood. It's like a release for the viewer. They see the evil in their lives violently destroyed. Payback. I mean you were there. Doesn't it feel good to watch them pay?

Fuck yeah, that's right. Crusher was beside them now, wiping sweat from his forehead, smearing his makeup.

I'm just not sure, Dunk said. Was it sadness he felt, swirling around in his stomach? That loneliness in his gut, all the more real now that he was back in Westinghouse. He was always leaving, wasn't he? The cult, Scusi's, even sobriety was a kind of departure. Now it was hard to feel like he had anything to add. Dunk swiped at his eyes to hide the moisture there.

So, what, Mick said, Crusher hugs them to death? Mick tells Dunk that a love story will evolve in flashbacks, and Crusher will find her, rescue her from the cult, take her to counseling. The film is pro-counseling and anti-cult. It's the fight between good and evil, vet and draft dodger. At one point, Crusher will grab an American flag off the flagpole and use it to parachute from the roof saying, *You motherfuckers don't deserve the flag!* It's pro-religion, as Crusher marries his long-lost love in the Catholic church at the end. It's about taking justice into one's own hands. It's about returning, not running away. It's about homecoming and slaying the monsters of one's past. It's about conquering, finally settling down. But most of all, Mick says, my audience wants an action film, not some feel-good shit.

No, Dunk said, That's not exactly what I mean.

What, said Crusher. You want me to cry?

Mick stood, slapped the two men on the back. Holy shit! That's it! You're Ron Crusher. These are people you know. It feels good to take them down, but it also hurts, so you shed a tear. One single tear. That emotion. Holy shit that's powerful! Dunk, you're a genius.

I mean, Dunk said, but stopped. That wasn't what he meant. It wasn't hate but confusion, not anger but a sense of loss. Not that he wanted all that again, his old life, but he didn't want it ripped apart. He didn't need to see its guts.

Set it up again, Mick shouted at the crew. We're doing another take.

◞

Dunk didn't bother to fold his shirts before he stuffed them into the trash bag. He'd spent the last week waiting for Robbie to leave before emerging to salute the sun. Evenings, Dunk watched movies at Mara's so he wouldn't run into Robbie coming home at night. Mara was disgusted that Dunk hadn't seen *Cool Hand Luke*, caught him up on Fellini, had him scrunched over with laughter at The Three Stooges. Movies, for Dunk, had been a revelation. He'd watched Bugs Bunny for the first time at eighteen and couldn't take his eyes away. Even now he was enraptured by the miracle of film. And yet, when the credits rolled, he was glad to return to conversations with Mara. She asked him to tell her stories not about the cult, but about his road-tripping life, about Novato, California where he hung with Sly and the Family Stone, and about the wilderness in Wyoming where he watched for fires and huddled through freezing nights. About Blue Fawn and her hippie magic. They'd talk until late and then he'd sneak back to Robbie's before sunrise while Robbie snored.

But today was moving day and Robbie had knocked on Dunk's bedroom door at noon and shouted, Gotta be out by 7 p.m. No hard feelings. Tough love, bro.

It was only five and Mara would pull up any minute, but Dunk was basically ready anyways. Two Hefty bags contained his entire world. The same ones he brought to Westinghouse from Scusi's, a reusable, disposable life. For the next few weeks Dunk would sleep on Mara's couch. He'd looked into hotels, still had his savings, but they wanted credit cards, deposits, and Mara said, Fuck, man. I have, like, this huge apartment and I don't even use the living room.

Dunk argued, but eventually agreed.

Nothing was ideal. But it was how the Earth worked, a deeper wisdom, a karmic law. Chance wasn't happenstance but a purposeful nudge in the right direction. Dunk glided through a slow yoga flow in the man cave, breathed in through the nose, out through the mouth.

It wasn't like he was totally stagnant. He had a job now, a contract. In trailer number two Mick had waxed poetic about his and Dunk's special connection. They vibed, Mick said. I sense a similar history, similar traumas behind us. I was raised Catholic, you know, Mick said.

Dunk wasn't one to argue. Especially not now when he needed a job.

Mick had clapped a hand on Dunk's shoulder and told Dunk they could help each other. Think *collusion* not *collision*, a phrase eerily similar to one of The Mover's mantras.

Now Dunk skimmed the pages of the script while he waited with his trash bags for his ride. *Give it up, Mover Roy*, Crusher said, in a final showdown, moments before he unleashed a Gatling spray at the cult leader. But The Mover responded with laughter: *Give it up? But I can't give it up. They believe in me. You believe in me. I asked for none of this. It's everyone else who has made all of this mine.*

For a dumb action movie, Dunk sensed a surprising depth.

He heard the screen door open and Mara called down.

Dunk didn't bother to lock the door behind him. He threw his bags in her trunk and lowered himself into the passenger seat.

Mara said, Punch it, Chewie, and they were off.

She snatched a pill bottle from the cupholder and wedged it under her thigh, resettled into profile behind the wheel. She said, Remember how you said you owed me for letting you sleep on the couch?

She peeled through the stop sign, turned onto Diamond Street, headed south. She said, So my boyfriend's like, being super shitty.

Did he do something?

No, she said, Nothing more than normal. He called. He's broke and he found out I sold a bunch of his drugs and he wants the money. And, I mean, he left the shit with me for fuck's sake. He has his own stash.

You've sold a lot?

Mara watched the road, drove with both hands on the wheel. She said, Sold. Used.

Fucking dealers, dude, Dunk said. We could hire some of the extras, threaten him.

I'm being protective, he thought.

I don't want her to have to hurt.

Mara shook her head, stared along the length of the road. He's such a fucking asshole.

You could just delete his number. Change the locks.

He acts like I'm so fucking dumb.

Call the cops on him, Dunk said. As if sobriety had made him a narc. A narc again.

Come on, man. Fuck that bullshit. I hate him, but I care about him. He said he'd kill himself if I leave and as much as I want him gone, I can't stand the thought of him dead. Maybe it was easy to rat out your family and run away. But we've been together five years.

Dunk said, Shit, Mara.

The car bounced in and out of potholes but both driver and passenger stared straight ahead, unflinching, looking at something beyond the sky as it met the end of the road.

Mara said, Fuck. I'm sorry. I know it's not like that. I just wanted to know if you could drop off the money later this week. I really can't face him right now.

They had to maneuver around the trailers downtown and park a block up the street because her apartment entrance was cut off by the film crew's trailers. They had to heft Dunk's luggage along the sidewalk and flash IDs at the lone security guard who checked his list, then waved them along. They clunked up the stairs to Mara's loft. The front room was spare with tall ceilings, a wide-open space with a shoddy bar made of an unhinged door on top of two bookcases. There was a thrifted couch that Mara pulled out into a hunched bed. There was a table with a briefcase on top. Mara snatched the briefcase and slid it back into her bedroom. She said, Home sweet home.

⌒

Dunk was up in the air again, looping above the valley with Robbie in his single prop. The producer, as anti-drone as he was anti-CGI, had hired Robbie to take a few aerial shots of the scenery. Extra cash to buffer his retirement. One camera was positioned in the windshield, another on the wing for less stable, more swooping visuals. Robbie flung the plane into tight loop-the-loops, showing off, joggling Dunk's stomach. Dunk was pressed to the wall and lifted, then weighted back to the seat. When Robbie cooled down, evened out, Dunk shouted over the noise, So how's the old lady?

Robbie said, Not so good if you call her *old*.

Dunk grunted.

Robbie said that he and Mimi were settled in for now. He sloped the single prop toward Main Street then flattened it out to strafe the drag.

Westinghouse was a flashback. Tucker's Hobbies, which closed in seventy-three, appeared to be back in business, it's six-foot model robot visible by the front door. There was the reified bakery that had fallen in the Obama years, a record shop. All appeared open and thriving. As they neared the town center, the Worlinger Department Store bloomed with a fresh facade, that swirled font so familiar but also a distant dream. People filed into churches wearing summer clothes even though it was October, and Dunk remembered that just fifteen minutes earlier when he stepped into the hangar there had been a sharp chill in the air. But maybe the producers could change more than the town itself, could alter the weather. Mover Roy had proclaimed he could do such things, had them out in their underwear at midnight one subzero winter. Push-ups in the snow, pretending the moon into sunshine. The powerful, the elite, were almost as limitless as they were cruel. Robbie banked the plane toward the cumulus breaths, and Dunk looked down once more at the falsity of it all.

Robbie said, You know how much they're paying me for this shit?

That was the last thing on Dunk's mind but Robbie told him anyways. Two grand a day. On top of the house rental. Just to fly around. He said, I bet you're raking it in too, huh? Must be cake. Tell them the mural goes a little to the left. Or like, the robes aren't white enough. Lucky motherfucker.

Dunk nodded. He said, It's a lot of work though. Like emotionally.

Robbie laughed and joggled the plane.

Dunk wanted Robbie to understand. He said, It brings a lot of shit up, dude. We used to hate those people.

We never *hated* them.

What they did to us. What they made us do.

Oh, come on, Robbie said. He lifted the plane higher, passed over farmland now. He said, That's our folks you're talking about.

We didn't have a choice.

You had a choice. You left. I stayed. Sometimes it's about more than just yourself.

Dunk shook his head. No one asked you to stay with them.

You think I could just cut bait and let them suffer?

Who let who suffer, dude?

Robbie sat silently for a while. He gripped the choke with both hands. He said, Dunk, man, do you want to know what it was like?

Dunk didn't, but Robbie explained anyway. He'd stayed throughout the investigation. He was questioned and he lied. He shredded papers. He said, While you were out there hootin' it up with your acid tests and shit, I had to go out and bury dad's pistol and he kept looking for it, kept saying he needed it. Just one bullet.

Dunk sank. He couldn't take it. It had always been too much.

Robbie said, You know they had to close everything. Cruisin', Worlinger? And all the money was frozen. *I* took care of shit. Did you want our parents to just rot in jail? Die on the streets? Cause I wanted them to have a second chance. Just like you.

Dunk opened his mouth and closed it. He sweated, but it wasn't warm. He'd escaped and turned them all in. People were dead because of Dunk, but also no they weren't. At what point are you responsible for yourself and at what point for everybody else? Who let who suffer?

The plane descended and as it finally bumped along the freshly mowed Church of Future Souls field, Dunk saw the main lodge just as he'd so often seen it, the compound sprawled around them and people in their white robes, cross pendants, pious eyes, and he was unsure if this was a flashback or the real thing, another version of his life where he'd faced the consequences of his actions, where he'd stayed.

༄

Mick met Dunk by the runway and clapped a hand on his back as he walked Dunk across the field and through the doors of the lodge. They'd recreated the sanctuary as well so that it once again breathed cultish energy. The pews were refinished, stained glass reinstalled, the pulpit etched with arcane symbols: the fish, the loaf of bread, the dagger. The shofar horn that Mover Roy used to call the service curled atop the altar, scarlet banners hung from the ceiling. A red carpet was unrolled as if waiting for Mover Roy to once again walk down it, barefoot, while the parishioners bowed and sang. What would The Mover preach on today? Another prediction for a second coming divinated during his ritualistic blunt session with the high-level protectors? And when that day's numerology failed to forecast the end of the world, what would come next? Another witch hunt, more punishments, more rituals? Crucifixion. The imitation Church of Future Souls made Dunk feel stupid for even once buying into The Mover's bullshit. Hypocrite. Liar. Murderer. But he could also feel the smooth wood beneath his butt, the slick polish of the pew which he'd slide down as a child, snug against his mom's hips.

Dunk floated through the room like an already drowned body. When a parishioner extra looked his way and nodded, Dunk was torn between returning the greeting and ducking Mick's arm to run. Mick said, What do you think?

It's good, Dunk said, Like the real thing.

I want to evoke a sense of wonder, Mick said, A sense of awe and fear. Do you feel that? What do you feel?

It wasn't awe. And it wasn't exactly fear. More of a familiar comfort cut by knowledge that Dunk had played a part in ripping all of it away. Before Dunk was old enough to take an interest in the outside world, he'd spend the social hour after service receiving head pats from parishioners, listening to his mom share recipes with other mothers, asking the other children if they wanted to hit the monkey bars before supper. Once, he felt happy here.

Come on, Dunk. What do you feel?

I feel weird, Dunk said, Confused.

He felt The Mover's stare, the judgment, danger, and blame.

Mick winked and nudged Dunk down the aisle to the back of the room and up to Mover Roy's old office, now filled with camera equipment and laptops, its window overlooking the imagined congregation.

Okay, Mick said, So, we shot the passion reenactment scene and I need you to tell me what I'm missing.

Dunk pulled back. I'm sorry. I can't. But Mick clawed onto him, held him in place.

Mick hit the space bar and the excerpt played on the screen.

The camera zoomed out from a bloody brow, a crown of thorns, revealed a face, then a body, splayed, oozing darkly from stigmata wounds, crucified above the congregation of white-robed parishioners. Dunk half recognized some of the faces. Protector Benjamin, Albert up for sainthood, his parents, and Robbie, maybe, slumped in the back. Dunk shook his head, attempted to blink away the past. Mover Roy appeared on the screen, except this wasn't the tidy slick-haired, pointy-nosed Mover Roy. This fictive Mover had greasy curls, pure black contacts instead of the kind blue eyes Dunk recalled. Mick patted Dunk on the back. He said, Evil, right? Wait for it.

The crucified parishioner cried out. Dunk could hear his pleas only faintly. It was a reenactment of a scene that had taken Dunk a thousand tokes to forget, and he no longer saw his mom there, no longer felt the comfort of being squeezed against her. As Mover Roy removed the whip from its ceremonial stone, Dunk felt the sting of the knots against his own back, heard the command of The Mover and then the congregation, chanting in his own ears. *Believe*, they said, *Believe*. The Mover on the screen was Whipping Out the Doubt. Between lashes, The Mover said, Did the Christ cry out when he was nailed to the cross? No, because he trusted his father just as you should trust me. Bleed your doubt onto the ground and refill yourself with faith.

Dunk scanned the rows of hooded parishioners, anything but watch more of Mover Roy's violence. He tried to see under the parishioners' hoods. The congregation watched. Silent. Faces in the shadows. Brother Lance, Protector Thomas. No one broke their gaze. Even the child ghost of Dunk, seated in a pew, was locked in on the violence, believed in it, supported the torture, the murder, the cover-up. Someone had to stop this.

Back then, Dunk was frozen. He couldn't do anything.

While the fictional Mover whipped away, a figure rose from the last row. It was him. It was Dunk. Not the young Dunk, but the adult Dunk. The rebellious Dunk. The questioning Dunk who stood in unholy blasphemy and put his hands up to his hood, ready to speak out against what he knew was wrong, to stop the beatings and violence. The standing man, Dunk, threw back his hood, and it wasn't Dunk, but Ron Crusher. From his robes he pulled out a Molotov cocktail of anointing oil, lit the fabric wick.

Mick grabbed Dunk's shoulders and yanked him back. He said, You're fogging up the screen. He hit pause. I'll take that as a good sign.

Dunk rubbed his eyes. His nose tickled and he wiped away a spot of blood. A side effect of years' worth of cocaine, a re-stimulation of his ages-old want.

But seriously, Mick said, What do you think? Anything I missed?

Dunk pinched his nose and stared into the screen. It was too easy. That was the issue. A Molotov cocktail. A barrage of bullets. A hand grenade. But it took more than that to bring down a cult. It took a lifetime of convincing yourself that what you did was right. Booze and drugs to purge the guilt from your body. And the truth was, it was never purged. It was always right behind him. The fear, the worry. It was his fault.

∽

After a few more hours reliving culthood through Mick's clips, Dunk was worn thin. He approached the Musician and the Poet's pad at dusk and could hear the music from the side-walk, a crunch of harsh noise at peak volume. He tapped on the door lightly. Maybe if they didn't answer it would be enough of an excuse to turn and walk away. But when he knocked again, the door inched open. It wasn't even latched.

The house was a mess of full ashtrays and empty beer cans. In the living room, the Poet and the Musician passed a blunt and alternated lines of cocaine which they drew from a tiny Kilimanjaro in the center of the coffee table. They didn't seem surprised to see Dunk. The Poet gestured to the couch behind him and, on his knees, bowed forward into the drug pile, gasped back up, Tarzaned his chest. Fuuuuuck! He picked up the remote and clicked down the music to a volume just above social. He said, You made it in the nick of time. We're running out. You brought more coke, right?

Dunk looked at the white pile from which the Musician scraped caterpillar-fat lines. It was at least half an ounce, a gross mountain to conquer between only the two of them. He looked at the Poet's eyes, sunken deep and bright-veined, his lips chapped and cracked, gnawed on, his face soulless. The two seemed more drug than human. They'd jumped the chasm to the strung-out side.

The Musician came up from his line and stood. He said, He who owns nothing is responsible for nothing. Give up your possessions and be free.

The Poet said, We strive for the light.

Dunk mumbled a sarcastic, Right on.

The tune changed, a chirp and oscillation of keys. The Poet whipped a red bandanna from his pocket and blew until the clog came unjammed from his nose and thunked out. He reached back toward Dunk with the straw. You want a bump?

Dunk shook his head. Overpowering thirst, but his mouth wasn't dry. He said, No, man. I don't do that stuff anymore.

The Musician said, You hear this shit? Listen. You gotta hear this.

The volume rose. Dunk said, Just a minute, alright?

The Poet said, Coke, man. You got the coke?

Coke?

The Poet said, Fucking Mara … but the music cut him off. It was guttural and then it was nasal. This is what they'd been working on, the Musician explained. They'd recorded as the Poet read through his portfolio of blank verse, twenty hours of words, and they'd sampled the sounds, finally filtering the speech into disparate patterns, notes and cadences. They called it *Nonverbal Poetry*. A back beat dropped, indecipherable spondees. There was, in the weed and cigarette haze of the room, something prehistoric to the noise, however modern the dual monitors, soundboards, and wires that produced the music. All that poetry reduced to meaningless vocalizations. All those words, languageless, like speaking in tongues.

The Poet asked, So, what's the word?

Dunk shrugged. Nodded. It's unique. He didn't know what else to say.

The Poet said, Not the music, man. We know this shit's good. It's fucking groundbreaking. Original AF. He hit the blunt and exhaled the sentence, I mean Mara.

The Musician handed back a rolled-up bill and Dunk waved it off. He thought about it for less than a second and felt the need to congratulate himself for not thinking about it longer, but then, he was thinking about it again and his need started to take hold. He shoved the need back down. He was on a mission. He said, She's good, dude.

And you're living with her now? Shit. I mean age is just a number and all, but she's so vain. I never thought she'd be into older dudes.

Dunk said, It's not like that.

The Musician said, Man, dude, you're chill as fuck, my man. Not a care in the world.

The Musician passed the blunt toward Dunk and Dunk nudged it away.

But just a warning, the Poet said. She'll fuck you over no questions asked. Flaky as hell too. I mean look at you. She's got you running *errands* for her. Manipulative. Watch out.

This has nothing to do with that.

The Poet cut him off, Speaking of errands. Deliveries.

The Poet opened his palm and waggled his fingers in a gimme sign. Dunk pulled out the fold of cash and slapped it to the Poet who flipped through the bills and dropped the stack on the table. He said, She's fucking ripping me off. That fucking bitch.

He leaned in again and snorted a couple lines. Came up snuffling. He said, Man, you old hippies, you all knew your shit. Share everything. Let the Earth guide you. All the squares these days are like *go to college. Plan for your future.* But you're like, fuck the future, fuck the past. It's the moment.

Dunk began to correct him. He wanted to tell the Poet and the Musician that it's all fun and games until the body breaks down, until your heart stutters, stops, takes your job, your fun, your will, your life. But as he formed the words, the Musician put on something new and cranked the dial. The clickety clack of trains, the pound of die presses, and numinous above it all, another hymn, hummed breathily, indiscernible words through a screen of shower noise.

Dunk shouted, I need to go. I need to head out. And then his own voice issued from the speaker, and he looked above him to see the microphone dangling from the ceiling. The speaker said, *Right on* in Dunk's timbre. The Musician hit a button on the sampler and their conversation played back. He made it repeat the words, *that fucking bitch*, over and over like a record skip.

The Poet leaned into Dunk's ear and said, I got something you can bring back to her. Hold on. And he walked away. The coke adopted a glow, and Dunk's face flushed brighter with each *fucking bitch* the machine produced, a combination of sound and anger building with each cuss of Mara. Dunk shouted, Can you turn it off? But nobody heard him.

The Poet returned with a photo, Ron Crusher in a power pose, dressed in spandex and a leather vest, his signature scrawled below it. The Poet leaned in again. Bet you didn't know she was into this pro-wrestling shit. She left it here and I really don't want it around.

Dunk snagged the autograph away and stood up. He shook. He said, Jesus, dude. It's for her fucking brother. Get a clue. And he moved toward the door, but his left foot slipped on a bottle and his hand caught the tabletop which catapulted coke into the air. The clumps of it chunked apart and scattered. And just like that, the music stopped. But Dunk was still moving, through the door, along the drive, out onto the sidewalk, and when he looked back, he could see the two boys blinking into the streetlight from the black gape of their doorway. A lot of talk from guys who were fenced in by addictions familiar to Dunk: coke, self-centeredness, good stereo equipment. A lot of talk but they'd never understand.

∽

Robbie called seven times over the next few days, but Dunk only had to tap *ignore* in order to move on with his life. Robbie texted things like, *Dog's Leg. Saturday at six. Just to check in. You better not be fucked up again.* But Dunk could swipe left on the screen and slide the message off to cyberspace.

Robbie had asked, What's your plan? And Dunk hadn't known he needed one until now. Sure, the Earth still moved him, but he had to have a direction, a destination. He tilted his metaphorical sails toward forgiveness, toward a moment of peace. Imagined himself in a backyard weeding a flower bed, hands veined in mud and the world silent around him. You've done nothing wrong. Let it go. Cut it out. Forget. Yes, he still lived in the same world, the same state, even the same town as his trauma, but Dunk's mindscape was his own.

Mara showed up at the compound with lunch, and together she and Dunk hiked from the bustle of the shoot across the valley and up the steep incline of the gorge where they crouched on a rocky overlook, sunk their teeth into tofu salad sandwiches and looked over the sprawl, the mostly leafless trees that sloped down to the creek. The quaking aspens shushed like water-seep in the wind. The only other sound came from scolding woodpeckers as they jetted tree to tree and pattered out quick rhythms. Dunk concentrated on the breaths between bites, the freshness of the air, pine with a hint of mustard. This was peace, or at least close to it, though he also saw remnants of war, strands of ancient Future Souls fence subsumed into an unhuggable oak, or a rock foundation now heavily mossed and rotted. There was a scuffle of leaves and Dunk twisted toward the intruder, but it was just a squirrel who flung the foliage around while gathering its nuts.

Mara broke through Dunk's daze. She said, I think I'm leaving.

Dunk watched Mara try to smile. He said, Right on. He nodded. When he picked up his sandwich and bit into the soft bread, the soy sauce and salt pinched his inner cheeks. The mustard instigated a pucker.

Mara stared off. She said, I mean for real. I don't think I can stay in Westinghouse anymore. I'm just gonna give all that motherfucker's shit away and take off.

Dunk nodded, mashed the bread in his mouth, choked it down prematurely.

She said, I should have done it a long time ago. I gotta do something for myself. I gotta do something besides numb myself.

Dunk couldn't stop himself. He said, He's an asshole.

Then why do I feel like I'm betraying him? Why do I feel like I'm doing something wrong?

Dunk gulped another bite.

I mean, you left, right, Dunk? All those adventures. All that excitement. Freedom.

Dunk repeated that word, Freedom. He put down his sandwich. Caught back up in his old hometown with a brother who didn't trust him, a brainwashed life relived through a film that mocked his trauma. The key wasn't to rid yourself of the past. That was impossible, but to reshape the narrative. Dunk not as the villain, but the hero. You've done nothing wrong, he told her. You leave and whatever happens when you're gone, whatever your boyfriend does, that's on him. Not you. You gave him a shot. Now it's your turn.

Come with me, she said.

Dunk opened and closed his mouth. When the film was done the town would be enveloped, once again, in all its Podunkness, and he'd have enough saved for a modest down payment, a yard. The garden. If Robbie would drop the bullshit, he'd have his brother over for dinner on the front porch. He said, I can't.

A heron racketed its shout up to the rocks where they sat, where Dunk in his sukhasana watched Mara's face go bitter, then sad, then force a smile like it just couldn't decide anymore what was emotion and what was expectation.

Dunk said, I think I can tell you that leaving was the best thing I ever did. He picked up his bottled water and drank. He remembered the first ride, a lucky yellow VW Rabbit crawling along the state highway with another young, lost soul who hoped to find his way out West. An ex-Catholic and a cult member, the pair of them unlikely, but somehow so similar. They talked about that dream of Westward, a couple dudes, newly men, jamming *Maggot Brain* while they leaned back in their seats two days later in the desert, stared into a deep and endless sky.

He said, But I still feel like shit about it.

Mara munched her sandwich. She pulled a flask from her pocket and apologized to Dunk before she took a slug. She said, Okay, man. If you could reinvent yourself, who, or what, would you be?

Dunk thought about it for a while. He'd been so many things, held so many jobs, but above all that he'd always existed as someone who could float with the current. He didn't have a drive, a vendetta. He said, Maybe I'd be Ron Crusher. You know, kick some ass, take some names. None of that philosophizing, or second-guessing. Nothing going on up here.

Dunk tapped his head.

Just do what the director says.

Mara spat crumbs. She said, Your scrawny ass?

I don't know, Dunk said. He hadn't ever tried to be anything. He'd enjoyed the land out West the most, pulling vegetables from the ground, pruning pot plants, that kind of thing. He said, I think I'll be a gardener.

Mara nodded.

Dunk laid back, one of the last warm days of the year.

♫

Mick put his hand on Dunk's head and told him to duck, but Dunk ran his noggin right into the stalactite. The cave was smaller than he remembered and now it was packed with camera equipment and crates of fake explosives. He caught hints of pot smoke, but there was no way those half-century-old joints still lingered. There were whiffs of the grips' cigarettes, the musty damp cool as he walked back toward the mouth.

It was Ron Crusher's cave now. The ex-cultist revenge-seeker hid his stolen arsenal in the cavern and, at one point, slaughtered a runaway sacrificial goat and roasted it over the fire for supper. Dunk didn't want to dig into that metaphor. Crusher slept there, but mostly he didn't sleep because at night he was out on reconnaissance or picking off cult members one by one.

Dunk mentioned the missing livestock to Mick. It used to be a farm, Dunk said. We had, well, I don't know how many animals.

I trust you, Mick said, I mean, that single tear—pure magic! But it's an action movie, he explained, and the budget was only enough for either explosives or livestock and of course explosions always win. They would have to add the animals in post-production. He winked, You just wait.

And then Mick stormed off waving flamboyant instructions to the cameramen.

Dunk wandered away from the shoot. Within the hour, Ron Crusher, garbed in the same white robe but now tattered and laundered in blood, would leap out of the tunnel, sprint to the cave, and post up there to fight off the final parishioner onslaught. Hundreds would be gunned down by Crusher, and the few that survived the bullet barrage would be forced into Death Grips, Elbow Drops, a weird amount of Diving Headbutts. Mover Roy would escape back into the tunnel, because, Mick explained, Sequels. And Crusher would plunge the detonator and reduce the buildings to rubble.

From the ridge Dunk watched the ant trail of crew members construct their scene. Soon, Mick joined him, hand on Dunk's shoulder, surveilling the progress.

What's up, Dunk? Mick said, Is something wrong?

Mick pointed to the set. The extras, the dead bodies getting their blood touched up.

Dunk shrugged off Mick's hand. Turned to Mick. Just something I've been thinking about with Crusher. This whole thing. Something off.

Off? Oh my god! It's the accent, isn't it? Or it's the robe? Should he have the left side overlapping the right?

It's the violence, Dunk said.

It was all so clear to him now. The violence came too easily, too simple a solution.

He said, You can't just blow everything up behind you and move on. That shit lingers. I tried. I should know.

Yes, said Mick, Your story. The infamous phone call. But think of it this way: Not as real violence, but a metaphor. A purging. Not what happens but what it makes you feel.

But what does Crusher feel? All that anger over all those years. What happens when it's done?

What happens? Mick queried the air. His phone chimed in his pocket. I have to take this.

When Mick walked away, Dunk stood in mountain pose and breathed, then worked through his asanas, greeted the sun.

∽

It was evening when the lighting was right for the final explosion. Dunk stood with Mick Jonathan and the rest of the assorted crew on the opposite edge of the gorge, far enough away that the cave was nothing but a flea hole, the church itself, an insignificant speck. There were prop bodies all around. A massacre. False. Impossible. Ridiculous.

Alright everyone, Mick said, holding the detonator above his head. The moment we've all been waiting for.

With his free hand, Mick clapped Dunk's shoulder. The crew, the actors, even Crusher, held up their phones, pointing in Dunk and Mick's direction, filming the two of them.

This moment calls for something special, Mick said. He held the remote between himself and Dunk. A metaphorical purge through art. The two of us: religious trauma obliterated with the press of a button.

Dunk hesitated.

Put your hand here, Mick said.

Dunk obeyed. His thumb hovered over the button.

Mick said, Just wait for the all clear.

The crew held their breath. A moment of silence.

The voice crackled affirmative through the radio.

Dunk's thumb trembled.

Count down from three, Mick said. Three, two, one.

Push! Mick said.

Push and be free.

Dunk smiled. He felt the director's thumb pressing his own thumb into the button. He pushed and the past erupted, then swirled slowly back to dust.

Part III: Captain Failure

Dunk bought a six pack for Mara's end-of-filming party, the first beer he'd purchased in a couple months. Modelo, nothing cheap. Not the swill he once drank. When he clunked the bottles onto the counter at the Circle K, he felt the eyes of everyone around him. He had to convince them this wasn't a relapse. It wasn't for him. He looked around the place, spotted the only other customer, a young woman in sweatpants and a hoodie with a bag of Cheetos and a forty. Nobody knew him. Nobody cared.

When Dunk entered Mara's living room, his bed was folded back into a couch form and on it sat three hipsters who leaned into the coffee table to snort their lines. The Musician shuffled through the records, pulled a couple out to stack on the pile he'd built. The Poet lay savasana on the floor. When Dunk passed above him, he said, with an affected British accent, My good sir! Would you tell me which way is up?

He's fucking zonked, my man. The Musician held up a tattered Herbie Hancock sleeve for inspection. Motherfucker ate a whole strip.

Disgust flitted through Dunk but he breathed acceptance back in. He said, Where's Mara?

The Musician said, He thinks he's Jeeves. Don't know where the fuck he got that from.

The Poet giggled and said, May I take your coat?

Dunk asked again if anyone knew where Mara was. Someone snorted something big from the table and shouted, HOLY FUCK!

RZA brought the ruckus, spread it through the air.

Dunk took the hallway through the kitchen where the Gaffer sat on the counter and stared into a crystal. The light ranged in fractal patterns on the wall. The Gaffer hit a blunt with his free hand and offered it to Dunk. He said, Have some life? His heavy locks of hair tapered over his shoulders. He said, Try it! Live!

Dunk waved him off, but the Gaffer kept stabbing the blunt at him. Something in it smelled sweet and crackled. When the Gaffer took another draw, it sparked. Dunk already had plenty of life and he wanted to talk about it with Mara, not some crackhead. The briefcase, Dunk noticed, was sitting on the stovetop, empty. Thousands of dollars' worth of drugs dissipated, booze evaporated. When all the drugs are gone, what is left but every mistake, every wrong action? And what if you aren't ready to face that? What if you need to live vacant, hollow? Dunk reached into his bag and set the six pack next to the Gaffer. A gift, he said, from the spirit world, and he walked outside unburdened. Alone.

But he wanted something now. He was moving toward it, not just floating stoned and timeless. On the porch he was packed in with the smokers, but when Dunk got to the railing he could see the city lights spread below him. It only took them a single day to tear down all the scaffolding, to return the storefronts to their original rust and filthy glass. The airport no longer swarmed with bigwigs, but was reverted to blinking control towers, a far-off glow. Somewhere out there was the compound, leveled. Scorched earth left to reseed, regrow.

He called her name. Mara? Mara?

He was answered by offers of marijuana, other drugs.

Drugs that eclipse memories, blur time, but now that Dunk had a goal, he didn't have time to waste.

He had to walk through the bedroom to leave, and on the way he noticed her closet left half open, empty except for the Poet's clothes. Her bed was stripped to the bare mattress. Her posters were ghosts with four corners of balled sticky tack. She was gone. Dramatic way to leave maybe, but how better to vanish? In an instant. In the middle of a party. Here, then only a slowly fading memory.

On his way out the record began to skip, *All you need is* love, *love*, love, *love*, love, *love*, love, *love*. The alternation of stressed and unstressed syllables, the stylus clicks, removed from the music, removed from Dunk.

Outside he shivered. A chill had moved in from Michigan, through Toledo, scraped its way down Seventy-Five, Thirty East, like a rust bucket dragging its exhaust. And if that weren't enough, as the wind slowed, the crows rustled by, shouted at the air, and Dunk ducked under the awning just in time as crow shit splattered, as they took off somewhere higher. Then he heard his name, Dunk, yelled into the caw of the rising murder. He heard it again. She said, *Up here*, but when he looked he didn't see anything except a shadow, above it, the obscured light of the moon. She said, Come around to the back. The fire escape.

It was Mara.

❧

She chugged from a jug of Carlo Rossi, the stuff of rotten guts and icepick headaches, stained-purple party teeth, and she sat on a blanket large enough to wrap around the both of them. Her duffel bag and backpack served as pillows. The moonlight tried to shirk the clouds and mostly failed, but they lay back anyways a couple feet apart, and Dunk tried to pick out the stars. The Big Dipper was there. He pointed. But then it was hidden. After another moment, Dunk said, I thought you'd left.

I did, she said. I took off this morning with a bottle of whiskey and I drank and drove around for a while sloppy as fuck, but nothing happened. I didn't die or crash or go anywhere at all. All of a sudden I was back on Main Street, like a mile from home. So, I thought, what the fuck. I guess I wasn't ready.

But you didn't go back, said Dunk. Not inside the house at least. You came up here.

No. *He* was in there. He keeps trying to apologize. I don't believe him, but I want to believe, you know. An asshole, but an asshole I know. Something like that.

Someone from below screamed Holy Fuck into the night and then others joined, a chorus of Holy Fucks howling at the dark. Mara offered Dunk some of the blanket and he draped it over one leg, then most of another.

She glugged from the bottle and gasped. She said, Maybe I'll have the courage to leave again when this is gone.

Dunk shook his head. You should just forget the wine, dude. It's not gonna help. And I'm not just saying that because I'm sober now.

She laughed. I know. Fuck.

Dunk nodded.

She said, Why the fuck can't I leave! She yelled it at the sky, at everything around them. She quieted and said, Come on.

Come with me?

Dunk said, Dude. You know I can't.

I know, she said. I know, I know, I know, I know.

And all this shit, Dunk spread his arms to envelope Westinghouse, its cults and capitalists, its druggies, artists, even the junkyard. All of this will still be here when you get back. Just a little bit different.

I know, She took another gulp. She said, Maybe I just feel like I need a sign. She let the bottle clunk down beside her, most of the way gone. She laid her head back on her hands.

Bottle rockets popped on the porch below, and a trail of sparks flew into the sky, then bloomed and skittered back to black. A bigger boom and a whistle. More static, more whooshes and blasts in the clouds.

They both leaned back and said nothing, watched the thin smoke wisp away, listened to the party crowd drift inside. Then, out of nowhere, a final bottle rocket screeched overhead, popped right above them and sparkled down. Dunk rolled onto his side to look at Mara. He said, There you go. That can be your sign. But Mara was already asleep.

∽

The sun shines on Mara's rooftop where Dunk wakes up, burritoed in a blanket, an empty bottle of Carlo Rossi at his side. And below him, in the street, semis attach to trailers, yank them toward the interstate and back West, a caravan of film-crew hangovers in airport-bound vans and rental cars. Flatbeds struggle south with scrapped sets of an imaginary Westinghouse. A Westinghouse that is no more. They're followed by actors and other bigwigs in tinted SUVs. Trash everywhere. Cigarette butts and empties, shattered glass and crumpled, annotated scripts. Then, silence.

It isn't until everyone's gone that Dunk stirs. He shakes his head and his hair fans out. He's too old for this. Too old to sleep on rough rooftops or on Mara's lumpy couch. Too old to be up late, unemployed and soul-searching with twenty-six-year-olds. Even if they're old souls. Even if Dunk is bored by people his own age with their retirements and insurance plans. But then again, what is age but whatever fragments of wisdom you pick up along the way? It's what you take with you and what you leave behind.

He lifts himself to his feet and moves through his sun salutation. He works his way through rooftop warrior, rooftop forward fold, and breathes his mind empty. He's as open to the world as a curious child and smiles as he knots the blanket around him like a cape. Next to the bottle he sees a set of keys, Mara's. He'll take them to her, suggest breakfast, maybe, something for her inevitable hangover. He's not hungover, not anymore, not ever again. For once, the day looks new, a live thing to cling to, not drink away or battle against. He clunks down the fire escape and each landing jolts his knees, but he keeps going. As he drops onto the empty brick lot, it hits him. The keys. No luggage. Mara is gone.

Dunk approaches the front of the building where a guy who must be the landlord jams a jingling ring of keys into the lock and mutters to himself. Dunk only wishes for a moment that Mara had said goodbye, but goodbyes linger and she needed to leave everything behind. Start fresh. The church bells signal the start of service, but besides the belfry's call, the tinkle of keys, and landlord's murmur, the day sits in still meditation. No traffic. No chatter. It waits.

Dunk looks for a garbage can, somewhere to leave the bottle so this man doesn't think it's his. He's beaten alcohol, not a single fond memory from the tannic reek. He sets it in the entryway of a blacked-out shop. Now, with the blanket cape around his neck, he's ready to vanquish the corny sneering villains of his imagination. The Robbies, the Mover Roys. He's a man who turned the corner into a wonderland of possibility. A breeze flutters past, the chill of winter in it, and it marionettes a crumpled paper across the sidewalk. He can smell the production crew's exhaust fading, this final reminder of a Westinghouse that used to be.

The church bells cut out and the landlord quiets and stops. He turns to Dunk, blinks. He says, Who the fuck are you supposed to be? Captain Failure?

Dunk smiles. Captain Failure, leader of Deadheads, the hippie hangers-on. It's humor and grandeur and irony all wrapped into one. It's nothing sad or frightening or angry. The man says, I don't got any money for you. Move along.

Dunk looks up at the apartment, and Mara's second-story windows are now a wall of glare. Dunk says, I don't need money, man. I just left some of my shit up there.

The landlord says, Of course. She had squatters. Fuck me. He returns to attack the lock once more with key after misfit key. Then he turns back. He says, I'll tell you what. You get me inside and you can grab your shit. I'll give you five minutes. And just *your* shit, right.

He returns to his muttering, Call in the middle of the night. Break the damn lease. Rent already late.

He kicks the metal door frame and the glass inside it wobbles.

Dunk shivers under his blanket cape, but the cold doesn't bother him so much. He's Captain Failure. He can survive a heart attack, a cult. He can inspire Mara and set her free. His real superpower though? Well, he can change the world. He can take the Westinghouse he's always known, the Westinghouse with cults and whippings and guilt and drugs, and he can transform it into a garden filled with sustenance, a bask in a spontaneous sun.

And that's the difference between himself and Mara, between now and when he ran away. Now he can also, just as easily, stay.

So, what do you say, bud? Should I get a locksmith out here or you gonna work some magic? The landlord looks Dunk up and down, judges the tattered hems of his corduroys, the lost button on his stained linen shirt. He sniffs in Dunk's direction. Dunk stinks like yesterday's slept-in sweat. Dunk just shrugs, then pulls out Mara's key ring. He says, Hold your horses, my dude.

Drug Magic

Now that Abe no longer shoots heroin, he sounds like a fifty-dollar self-help seminar and the problem is I've seen this all before. The problem is that my life these days is a series of dips and dives while my brother, despite his past, keeps thriving. The problem is he won't shut up about it. Abe tells me it's not luck but Drug Magic, that all his previous wrongs have undergone a reversal. He says, "No, Mags, Drug Magic's not pulling a rabbit out of a hat. It's like you ask the universe for what you need, and you get it."

He lies on his creeper under a Honda Civic ravaged with rust. He grunts, punches. A bolt cracks.

He says, "Hand me the breaker bar, Mags."

I don't hand him the breaker bar because who the hell knows what a breaker bar is and because I'm headed off to the community college where I'm working on my nursing degree so I can one day move beyond in-home healthcare, beyond a raggedy-ass house on the East Side. I could really use some Drug Magic now that rent is due and my last charge, Gertrude, is dead. I corner my Buick and beg the universe like Abe's instructed, but nothing happens. I slow down in front of Cash Max Loans, but I'm not that desperate yet.

ᔐ

Abe says being desperate is the key to Drug Magic. He says, "The magic is that if you're desperate enough, you make it happen. Like if you need dope, you steal that shit."

To me, the magic is the way these rusted Hondas appear and then vanish, how they beep in on a reversing tow truck and braaap their way out just inches from the ground, how Abe counts his stacks of cash in the whorl of exhaust. Drug Magic to me is the way the sink piles up with dishes and oily tools while I work night shifts, but when I wake up in the afternoon it's scrubbed down to shimmers. It's why the hell I even let Abe stay here in the first place after all the shit he's put me through.

In the letter I wrote to Abe while he was still off at rehab #3, I included an itemized list of his transgressions. Besides the credit card he stole, the arguments and lies, there was his carelessness as the family fell apart.

I remember the Christmas when I clenched my jaw while aunts and uncles praised Abe's recovery. That was after rehab #1 when Abe became Buddhist and refused to get a job. While I studied and barista-ed part time, Abe swiped small bills from the vacation fund and smoked pinners in his basement bedroom. While Mom and Dad argued over mortgages and medical bills, Abe chanted his oms on the couch. After rehab #2, the one led by bodybuilders, he chugged protein shakes and said things like, "The only way out is through." He told Mom "Winners never quit" while she tried to pack her bags, fit her life into the trunk of her car, and "Pain just makes you stronger" as she took off to Atlanta to live another life. Dad didn't know what to do either. Insurance was too high. Everyone was broke. So Abe and Dad just shouted, and Abe punched holes in walls, while I studied, eavesdropped, cried, from my bedroom down the hall.

When I finished writing that letter, I rewrote it without the wet smudges. I pulled up the blinds and there was the gray Ohio world, family-free. A week later I skimmed Abe's response, then tossed it on the dining-room table, lost it under piles of bills and ads, headed out to my night shift watching Gertrude fade away.

ᔆ

I used to talk to Gertrude while I checked her vitals and fed her meds through sleepless nights. I'd list the bones of the body, pose practice quiz questions about neurotransmitter deficiency in Parkinson's patients. While wiping her ass, I'd ask, "What's the cause of most lawsuits involving nursing professionals?"

On good days, Gertrude would say something like, "Probably wiping butts with that cheap-ass TP." But as time went on her words became gurgles and she sat dead-eyed in front of the TV while Archie Bunker screamed racist slurs at the Jamaican lady doctor who only wanted to help.

It was about midnight and she was still watching *All in the Family*, gurgling away when I got the call from Abe that he was out of rehab, about to catch a flight to Cleveland. I was nice. I said, "How the fuck did you get my number?"

He said, "Didn't you get my letter?"

There was a quiver in his voice, and I saw my chance to break him.

He said, "I've got nowhere else. You can say no. You should say no." A quaver, a sob.

"Don't fucking cry," I said, "I'm busy watching a woman die."

"I'll owe you. I'll pay you back. I'll pay you back double. I wish I didn't have to call you."

Actual tears, I could almost hear them plop.

Abe said, "They're hooking me up with a temp agency. Four weeks and I'll have a paycheck."

What was I doing with my life anyways but passing meds to a dying lady? I didn't even have friends, really. All I had was the bubble of Tonya, the first-shift caretaker who replaced me every morning. When Tonya swung into the room with a "How are we feeling today?" I went to Walmart and bought a safe. At home, I poured all the beer I couldn't finish down the drain, drunkenly shoved the entire craft room into the closet to make space for the inflatable mattress. When the air pump stopped working, I blew into the nozzle until my cheeks stung.

∽

Now Abe's upgraded to a queen-sized bed and a box spring that he scored from the VOA, his first real bed in one hundred days of sobriety. He works his temp job at the thermostat factory in the evening and fixes up cars in his free time so he can sell them to the types of shady dudes who hang out in the Taco Bell parking lot at midnight, engines bare beneath the streetlights. Now that Gertrude's dead and I'm scrounging for cash, I sit in front of the TV, flip through note cards over muted *All in the Family*. It helps me remember the answers.

After a year of third shift, I can't sleep at night. I squint my way through the front door in the morning to the screech of metal, Abe sanding paint bubbles to the rust below. He calls it patina, but it's just corrosion. Drug Magic is the car parts that materialize in the yard without my permission. It's tires that lean against the garage and a dude I don't know in a hoodie at the end of summer watching Abe buff the driver's side door to a linseed oil shine. There are new engines weighing down the crumbling shells of Volkswagen hatchbacks, glasspack exhausts revved by fender-bendered beaters. Abe says, "Just like my ugly mug. You can't see the Magic cause it's under the hood." He knocks his fist against his goofy head.

I say that maybe I should've just gone to rehab instead of college, gotten Drug Magic instead of this useless degree.

Abe straightens to a lanky tower with hunched shoulders, "Ok, Mags, what's up?"

I say, "Shit, man. Gertrude's dead and I'm broke." A tear dribbles down, tickles my upper lip. He moves like he's about to hug me, but when he looks over his shoulder at his friend, I step back. I wipe my face on my sleeve. I tell him I'm trying to do what's right, too, but Gertrude had to go and die and now I'm short on rent and nothing's really going right at all.

Abe pulls a wad of cash from his pocket, an inch thick of doubled-over bills. He used to tote folds of money like this when he was dealing. I remember Christmas '07, just before rehab #1 when he pulled off hundreds and low-fived them into everyone's palms as a gift and then a couple hours later, excused himself to tip from the toilet to the floor, smashed his head on the linoleum from a heavy-handed shot.

Abe peels off some money. I hold up my hand. He's already paid off his debt, his half of the bills. I can't ask for more. He says, "It's the least I can do. Like I was saying, you put your need out there and the universe provides."

I want to ask him if the universe cares that the cash is un-taxed, coming from nefarious characters who hide their faces, leave cigarette butts in the yard. But I need the money. Maybe this is the Drug part of the Magic, the part that doesn't ask questions, slips what you need in your pocket without a word while trying to choke back the shame.

〜

But the magic persists, expands, becomes real. I pay rent and the next day get a call about a new client, Zechariah, at $15 per hour. His beard hangs down to his belly button, eyes set into the skull, and he's hardly any work at all because when I give him his prescription Oxycontin pills he becomes kind for a while, then passes out.

When I get home, Abe's futzing with a puzzle of engine parts laid out and labelled with marker-scrawled masking tape on the garage floor. He stands to face me, all six feet of him, skeleton and muscle within billows of stained coveralls, the sunken cheeks and eyebrows.

He says, "They say you can't have recovery without honesty, and you can't adjust without trust."

I bite my lip, feel the sleep drain from me. I say, "Trust? Abe, what the fuck did you do?"

"I didn't *do* anything," he says, "Stinkin' thinkin'. I've been falling into it." He pulls his hand from his pocket, in his palm, cigarette-pack cellophane, indiscernible pills. He says, "I bought the car from the junkyard and found them beneath the back seat. They usually search before I get the cars. One time Randy found a wallet, another time, a human finger. How crazy is that?"

I tell him crazy is my brother with a crinkled baggie full of drugs when he hasn't even seen six months clean. I tell him crazy is me thinking I can trust him. "Trust is rust," I say, "trust is fucking out the window."

"Mags," he says. "I didn't do it. The bag's still sealed."

Then we are on the road. After he handed me the pills, we almost hugged again, but he broke the awkwardness with an ask. A clutch assembly in Dayton and he says he needs a friend to come along. He needs someone to keep him in check, so he isn't alone with his thoughts.

He puts on Neil Young's "The Needle and the Damage Done," breathes this melody in with all its irony, shifts into fifth and pushes the gas to rumble us through the countryside. Corn turned to chaff and husks on either side. We belt out the lyrics while the sun rises in his eyes, red in his cheeks, hands stable on the wheel.

We stop in Westerville for barbecue and Abe says he's buying. He says, "Have a beer. For real. I'm cool. And you're not even driving." But I don't have a beer. I add my sober days to his, suck barbecue from my fingers, soak napkins with the sauce. He says nothing about Drug Magic, maybe because we don't really need anything right now, maybe because the only thing we want is the clutch, and we're already on our way to get it.

∽

Drug Magic is how old man Zechariah is fine once he takes his pills. He's a jittery, helpless grump through the day, but when I pull the bottle from the cabinet and rattle out an Oxy he calls me Honey. He says, "Honey, you're such a blessing."

Drug Magic is how, when he starts to have trouble swallowing, I crush the Oxycontin with the back of a spoon, stir it into his orange juice. It's the way the pills make him sleep through the night so that I can clean the house and then nap till sunrise.

He bitches at the TV and I bring his Oxy-orange, stick a straw in his mouth. I wonder how much this job would worry Abe, how far down he would spiral with that pile of powder in front of him. Zechariah chokes, spits the juice on the floor, claws the glass from my hand burbling orange on his lap. "You're trying to kill me! I seen you put that shit in there."

I hold back a *fuck*. "I'm sorry." It takes a half hour to calm him down. I mop up the floor, pour his pills on the counter, and flick through them pile to pile. Not enough left to get him through the week. My brother is a junkie and my coworkers know it. So many mornings I've bitched to my replacement how living with a recovering addict worries me, how I'm always questioning a reddened eye or a clenched jaw. These things run in the family. Now the bottle will be a pill short and who do you blame?

In the morning, I have to park down the street. I come home to a house I don't recognize, grass prairie-ing around mounds of metal, hubcaps smashing the yard down to yellow, car bodies on blocks cover every spot of concrete. There are clangs and clashes coming through the garage door. With clinicals, work, and school, I don't think I've seen Abe all week.

I slam cupboard doors in the kitchen, not a coffee cup in sight. I curse Abe as I stomp through his bedroom snatching up mug after dredge-bottomed mug.

Back in the kitchen, I stop still and rustling, hands full of dirty dishes as he twists a butter knife into a greasy alternator. He says, "Mags, you look like shit."

I decide to break his smile. A cup cracks as I slam it on the counter. "For fuck's sake, Abe, can you at least keep your grimy-ass car shit in the garage?"

"I'm sorry. I couldn't find my flathead. I've just been picking up all these side jobs since they laid me off." He gestures with the alternator. "Cash."

"Laid you off? Fuck. Laid you *off*?"

Abe smiles that Drug Magic smile, "No worries. I have a list of twenty people wanting oil changes. I was gonna call my business Abe's Lincolns, but I don't really work on Lincolns. Got a Caddy in the garage now."

I say that he should call his business Homeless Hondas because there's no way in hell I'm letting him run an illegal mechanic's shop out of my house.

Abe says, "Come on," and I see it now, that hope boiling in his mind, that need to repair, to keep working until he's too tired to work. To take something ruined and make it hum.

"No way in hell," I say. "And this shit better be all cleaned up by the time I'm home."

Abe asks, "When is that?" and I let the door answer for me.

∽

I once again count Zechariah's pills while he coughs and sputters. His brain stem is corroded, his memories, his vocabulary, eaten by disease. I'm here because he has outlived friends and family, left them all behind. I'm here because he pays me, or his estate does, or whatever. It's business. I have a contract with his daughter who moved down South and never calls.

Tonight, though, I have that crinkled cellophane Drug Magic in my purse. I cut the plastic and Morphine tumbles out. It's not Oxy, but the pill's still powder and it dissolves into OJ and Zechariah will sleep and no one will know the difference. Zechariah drinks through the straw without question this time.

I sit with him until his eyes droop. He says, "Honey" and mumbles off to sleep. I manage the transfer lift from chair to bed and he snores as I tuck him in.

Tomorrow, I'll tell Abe there's a way we can do this. I've been thinking. We can't run a garage out of the house, but, I'll say, filled with goodwill and enthusiasm "*where there's a will…*"

He'll say something equally vomit-inducing like, "If you need it, the universe will deliver," and I'll roll my eyes and try not to slap him. He'll say, "you see, Mags? This shit works! Drug Magic" and I'll just say whatever. Fuck it. He'll give me that grin and we'll clean up the house together. We'll sweep up the rust, mow the yard, plant a damn garden. I don't know. We'll figure it out. We need to, and we'll use that need like a drug.

Acknowledgments

These stories only span about five years of actual writing, but I've split my headspace between reality and Westinghouse, Ohio for over a decade. I wouldn't have survived Westinghouse without the help of passionate and driven friends: Aaron, Addison, Anne, Chris, Forest, Hillary, Jon, Jordan, Sam, and everyone else who I don't have space to name here. I'm glad we escaped.

And then there were the years when I learned to talk about Westinghouse. Rebecca Schiff, Lawrence Coates, and Jackson Bliss: you guided me into new language, fresh forms that allowed the stories to flow. Thank you, Angela, Brenna, Chad, Joe, Joe, Matt, Matt, Michelle, Neeru, Turner, and everyone else who shared BG with me.

Thank you to the following editors who saw the hope in my Westinghouse stories and published them in slightly different forms: Diego, Laura, Joe, Keith, Meagan, Michelle, Tad.

And special thanks to the Elizabeth George Foundation, PEN America, Vermont Studio Center, and the DC Commission on the Arts for their support over the past few years as I polished this manuscript.

I couldn't have asked for a better editor than Kevin Breen who saw the beauty, comedy, and pain in Westinghouse and helped me draw it out. Sometimes, during rewrites, I wondered if you could read my mind.

And to those who inspired me early on: Andrew, Bob, Cynthia, Elizabeth, Jamison, Norman, Steven, and everyone else I worked with at the branch.

John Thrasher: I've dreamed of pairing your art with my words. Thank you.

To the DOW crowd who saw bits and pieces of Westinghouse before I knew it was Westinghouse: Allison, Beth, Bill, Jason, Jason, Jennifer, Mark.

I wouldn't have made it this far without the encouragement of my DC people: Andrew, Andrew, Kristi, Lauren, Lena, Martin, Mary.

Thank you, Boyd and Cindy: the best of literary citizens.

My family has saved me again and again. You keep me coming back, keep me grounded. Too many names to name; too much love to leave on the page.

And of course, Llalan, thanks for the many drafts you've read, and for all the rest.

About the Author

Nick Rees Gardner is a writer, critic, writing teacher, and beer and wine monger. His books include, *So Marvelously Far*, (Crisis Chronicles Press, 2019), an accounting of addiction and recovery in the Rust Belt; and *Hurricane Trinity* (Unsolicited Press, 2023), a climate change novella. He has received support from the Elizabeth George Foundation, Vermont Studio Center, the De Groot Foundation, and DC Commission on the Arts and Humanities. He lives in Ohio and Washington, DC.

9 781960 593030